MOTHER

C.M. ADLER

Witches of Grimm

C.M. ADLER

Witch in the Woods
(Prequel)

Mother
Kissing Crows
True Love
Pretty Things
Blood on my Shoe
The 28th Piece of Gold

www.QueensAndCrows.com

Mother: A Mother Gothel Tale
Witches of Grimm Book 1
Copyright 2021 by Christine Nielson/CM Adler
All rights reserved.

This is a work of fiction. Names, characters, places and incidents either are the product of the author's imagination or are used fictitiously. Any resemblance to actual persons, living or dead, events, or locales is entirely coincidental.

Creative Contribution by C. Haggerty
Cover art by Monika MacFarlane
Interior Book Design by Christine Nielson/CM Adler

Published in the United States
EBOOK ISBN: 978-1-950546-17-6
PRINT ISBN: 978-1-950546-18-3

Library of Congress Cataloging-in-Publication Data
Available upon Request

Pocket Pimp Publishing, LLC
1027 S 500 E K202
Heber City, Utah 84032
www.queensandcrows.com

For Dylan

ONCE UPON A TIME

Once upon a time there was a beautiful, sweet girl who grew up near an enchanted wood. She was the delight of her father, the most precious gem of his heart.

And one evening in spring, on her sixteenth birthday, she clutched her infant daughter to her chest and ran for her life…

THE ONLY TRUTH

Cerelia wasn't as afraid of the darkness or the blood running down her legs as much as she was afraid of the baying of her father's two favorite hounds. She refused to think about what they would do to her if they caught her.

What they would do to her baby.

She scrambled along the shore of a small sea, clutching her swaddled newborn to her chest against the chill of late fall. She tripped over some driftwood, landing on her knees on the smooth rocks. Somewhere in the back of her mind, Cerelia knew that it should hurt. But to her body, ravaged by childbirth, the jolt in her knees brought nothing but a faint echo of pain.

She struggled to get back to her feet, slipping on the rocks and weak from the loss of blood. For a moment, she felt like giving up. Maybe her father, the captain of the king's guard, would forgive her enough to call off the hounds and make it a quick death with his axe.

If they caught her, surely that would be the greatest mercy she could hope for.

She steadied herself on her knees, allowing a wave of dizziness to pass. Lifting her baby from her chest, she peered at the tiny face, the perfect little nose, and smiled and cried at the same time. Then she held her breath, watching to see if the baby was still breathing.

"My beautiful girl." Cerelia kissed her baby's cheek in relief after she felt her chest expand. She was weak but alive. "I will save us. I promise."

The stretch of forest in front of her was somehow darker than the one she had just come out of. Darker and full of magic. It was an enchanted wood, one that had fed Cerelia's childhood with stories of witches and goblins.

She had nowhere to go. She didn't want to run. She wanted a chance to explain it all, how it had happened while her father had been gone on a campaign in the king's name, taking her betrothed with him for months to defend the borders of their kingdom. In their absence, she had fallen in love with a commoner, a woodcutter's son who often delivered a supply of cut logs to the castle.

Love was turning out to be a very fragile and complicated thing. Until this night, her father had called her the 'gem' of his heart. Until this night, she had thought she was going to run away with a woodcutter's son and live happily ever after.

But those had all turned out to be lies, and the only truth that remained was that Cerelia had never known what love was until she held her child in her arms.

And she would go through any form of torment, brave any threat, to save her precious daughter.

Behind her, the small hunting party broke through the trees that separated the king's castle and surrounding city from the seashore. Two soldiers of the royal guard carried torches and swords. They wore armor, probably rallied from their posts when her father had discovered she'd run. Her father himself led the trio, standing in front with his favorite battle axe in hand.

The hounds bayed and ran toward her, the soldiers watching from their position near the trees. Cerelia only had time to realize that they were waiting for the hounds to do their part before her father and his soldiers bothered to trek across the rocks to reach her.

With a surge of fear, Cerelia made it to her feet and ran along the shoreline toward the enchanted trees. She hoped that her father's hounds would sense the magic and not dare to follow.

The rocks ended abruptly where the stretch of beach turned into cliffs and a small stream emptied into the sea. Tall conifers lined the beach and the cliff edge, drawing the boundary between the world of mortals and the world of magic. Cerelia scrambled up an embankment and across that boundary, hobbling as fast as she could in her weakened condition. She followed the stream where it cut into the trees, bubbling softly like a lullaby.

Soon her strength gave out. She fell to her knees at the edge of a clearing, an abandoned cabin on the far side. It was shelter, but it was too far for her to even crawl.

She kissed her baby's small face, her little hands. Even having been close to Cerelia's body, the baby felt cold. "I'm so sorry. This is as far as I can take us. I'm so sorry."

Then Cerelia remembered everything she'd ever learned of magic and spells as she spoke to the forest. It wasn't much. She had never fancied herself magic, but true desperation had its own power.

Her voice was a little more than a whisper. "Please, by the law of three, protect us. I give you my heart and my soul that safe we may be."

The hounds bayed. Cerelia couldn't tell how close they

were, their voices amplified through the trees. She slumped over her baby, her cheek pressed to the tiny head.

Something fluttered around her head, then sharp little teeth nipped at her hair. For Cerelia, it felt distant, as if it were happening to someone else. All that existed for her was the fading warmth of her child, the torn throbbing inside her body, and the icy breath of the night.

With the world fading away, Cerelia remembered a song her mother sang to her when she was a small child. It was the last thing she would give her daughter:

> *Hush now, darling; close your eyes,*
> *Dream yourself a thousand lives.*
> *One life of true love; one life of power;*
> *One life of kissing crows*
> *in a witch's crumbling tower.*
> *One life on a pirate ship with chests full of gold,*
> *And one life in a land where you'll never grow old.*
> *Sleep now, darling; close your eyes.*
> *Dream of a world with no goodbyes.*

As she sang the final syllable, she thought she heard the dogs sniffing around the edge of the clearing. The ground beneath her grew warm, and it rumbled.

Cerelia held herself up from the ground with one arm, cradling the baby in the other. Beneath her, a vine pierced up through the earth and shot through the baby and into Cerelia's chest. Before her heart could beat again, the vine wrapped around it and tore it from her, pulling her heart and her precious baby girl with it down into the earth.

1

GREAT AND DIRE CONSEQUENCES

Maia stumbled out of the servant's entrance and headed toward the village. She could hardly see through her tears, making her way through the spring-chilled front gardens by memory.

Lord Graves was evil. Pure evil. She had never believed that any human could possess such absolute cruelty. She knew he was more than selfish, a petty little man with a fragile ego. She had expected Lord Graves to be disappointed and stern, but not so calculating and absolute.

And Tom. He was supposed to love her. He had told her over and over again in the whispers of a precious secret. How could he stand by while his father accused her of such vile things? How could he stand by while his father demanded that she *die*?

Well, she was about to even the score. She would let the entire village know how dark Lord Graves's soul really was, how completely rotten.

Maia reached the town square while the villagers bustled about their days. She stepped up on the stone dais that stood beneath a magical archway in the center of town. It was a flat square slab of stone with iron arches starting at each of its four corners and meeting at the top with a round moon finial as the final detail. The arches were two flat bars spaced apart as a frame for the leaves and roses that scrolled between them.

The arch had been a gift from the blacksmith who had been one of the founders of the village generations ago, a man whom Maia had only heard of in local legends. One such legend said that after the archway had been erected, the goddess of the moon had come down and blessed it with eternal love and fertility. The legend also said that those who broke a promise that they had made beneath the arch would suffer great and dire consequences.

It was a favorite tradition for all couples to be married beneath it. Some even traveled great distances to access what they believed was binding love magic.

Unfortunately, Maia could vouch for the fertility part. But eternal love? That part was proving to be an absolutely horrible lie.

She just hoped that the great and dire consequences part was true.

Standing tall, her bare feet starting to ache with cold on the icy on the stone, she cupped her hands around her mouth and shouted, "Villagers! All! Hear ye!"

They paused, looking at her with a mix of curiosity and confusion. Maia had grown up with them, born in a house at the edge of the village and raised as if she belonged to each and every one of them after her mother had died of the pox. They carried their baskets full of baked goods and pulled their handcarts loaded with wood and leathers to the edges of the stone dais.

"My friends...my family," Maia began, fighting more tears. "I have been wronged. By our own Lord Graves."

"Oh, dear child." The village seamstress, Doni, pressed her

hand over her heart, her face pinched with worry. "What has happened?"

Maia wiped her nose on her sleeve. "I am with child. Tom's child. He promised me here beneath this sacred arch, that he loved me and would cherish me always. And now," she hiccoughed as she swallowed a sob, "the Lord Graves has turned me out of his house and threatened to hunt me down with those two insufferable thugs he calls his guards. He says I'm lying."

"You're certain you're with child?" the midwife, Catherine, stepped onto the stone. She stood beside Maia and pressed a hand on her shoulder, her face tight with worry. She looked at Maia closely, examining her.

Maia nodded. "Yes, I'm sure. I think five months now."

"Why have you not come to see me, my dear? Oh, you are certainly starting to show." Catherine patted Maia's little belly before she gathered the girl in her arms. "It is my job to care for you. I'll make sure you bring a healthy babe into this world, no matter who the father is."

"No matter who the father is?" Maia pushed herself out of the woman's arms. "It's Tom. I just told you that. He said he loved me, but the coward won't stand up to his bully of a father. Lord Graves accused me of—"

Maia hesitated, looking at the crowd. Fear dried up her tears. Where she had expected love and sympathy, there was nothing more than a tired apathy. A few of the villagers on the outskirts of the gathering turned and walked away, returning to whatever task they had been doing when she had interrupted them.

This was worse than she had hoped. She had expected questions and judgment, but overall she had expected the support and comfort she'd had her whole life. She'd been in all of their homes, cooked their food, washed their linens, and cared for their children when they were sick. She'd even lived with a few of them until Lord Graves offered her an appointment in his household when she was big enough to carry a full bucket of water by herself.

She hadn't expected them to just abandon her. Somehow that hurt more.

Like Catherine, they didn't believe her. She could see it in their pinched brows and in the furtive restlessness of their gazes.

"Accused you of what?" Doni raised an eyebrow. The village seamstress had been the first to take Maia in after her mother died. Maia would have hoped that she, of all the villagers, would be on her side.

Maia stepped away from the two women, a heavy feeling of dread settling in her stomach. This was not going how she thought it would.

Before Maia could answer, a shout echoed down the hill from Lord Graves's great stone house.

"Witch! She's a witch! Stand back!" It was Lord Graves himself, brandishing his favorite scepter and a new pair of pumpkin-colored pantaloons. Tom marched down the hill beside his father, flanked by the pair of household thugs in leather doublets that Maia had expected.

Maia didn't have to look around her at her fellow villagers to know the emotion that rippled through them. This was the one thing they were afraid of more than anything else, even though not one of them had ever seen a witch. It was a fear that had come with their first bedtime story.

Witch! She's a witch!

She felt the fear in them the same way she felt a breeze, by a subtle shift in the temperature and a chill down her spine. She heard them shuffling back on the cobblestones in the square, giving Maia a greater berth. Even Catherine and

Doni stepped down from the stone dais and out from under the beautiful iron archway.

Maia was alone.

Tom entered the square uncertainly, a pained expression on his face. He avoided Maia's eyes and scuffed a toe on the cobblestones.

Lord Graves, however, couldn't have been more self-righteous in his arrival. He tucked one hand in the belt that held his jingling money bag and raised his scepter with his other. "This *girrrrrl* here, standing before you, is a witch! She seduced my only son, my heir, my pride—Tom—" he pointed at the boy with his scepter, "—with her love potions and her spells. She—"

"You lying sack of gargoyle fodder!" Maia screamed back, her voice dropping as she choked on fresh tears. "Tom loves me! Not because of potions or spells, but because he…loves *me*. He stood right here under the sacred arch and told me that he loved me! Didn't you, Tom? Tell them."

Tom opened his mouth to speak, but his father cut him off.

Lord Graves's tone was low but loud enough to echo in the open square. "Yes, tell them, Tom. Tell them how she slipped her love potions into your stew and tricked you into believing she was beautiful. How she convinced you to give up the future of your family to lie with her. Tell them, Son."

Tricked you into believing she was beautiful? Through the overriding fear and hurt from Lord Graves' accusations that she was a witch, that she had used magic to trick Tom into loving her, those words stung.

But not as much as Tom's silence. The man—no, Tom was not a man, he was nothing but a nasty little boy cowering in his father's shadow—stood by with an expression of bewilderment on his face.

Maia looked around at the villagers gathered in the

square. Their faces had fallen into skeptical frowns, a few of them starting to look angry. One of the farmers adjusted his grip on his pitchfork and the blacksmith hefted his hammer.

She looked at Tom again, begging him with every part of her soul. Her voice trembled. "Tom?"

Tom pinched his lips together and glanced with fear at his father. Then his eyes burned through Maia and he became the embodiment of utter betrayal. "Witch."

Lord Graves raised his scepter and turned Tom's word into a rally cry. "Witch! Witch!"

The two thugs flanking Lord Graves called out. "Witch!"

Something round thunked the back of Maia's head. She reached up to rub her head as a rotten potato rolled unevenly along the cobblestones and stopped at Lord Graves' feet. Another hit the back of her shoulder and Maia spun around as Doni lifted another from the basket of pig feed on her arm.

The seamstress and the midwife stood with the other villagers. The scowls on their faces very clearly told Maia whose side they were on.

"Witch!" Tom's voice was now as loud as his father's.

"Witch! Witch!" The farmer pounded the end of his pitchfork on the cobblestones and the blacksmith smacked his hand against the flat of his hammer as they chanted along with Tom and Lord Graves. Doni and Catherine stomped their feet as they joined the men, then all the villagers, down to the candlemaker's bumbling toddler, took up the cry. "Witch! Witch!"

They started to close in. Maia was frozen in disbelief.

Lord Graves pulled his hand from his belt and twitched his fingers as a signal to his two leather-clad guards. "Seize her."

Half blinded by tears and panic, Maia hopped down from the archway and ran straight into the villagers. Someone ripped a handful of hair from her head as she pushed her way through the crowd. Her fear dulled the pain. She passed the banker's and the leather smith's and made it to the cottages that edged the village. She could hear the guards' boots pounding on the cobblestones, and then the softer sound of them running on the ground where the cobblestone ended.

The cottage belonged to Doni, the seamstress. Maia knew it well, having tended to the chickens and pigs whenever Doni fell ill and had to stay abed. The chicken coop was closest to the village, and the chickens *bawked* and fluttered their wings with Maia's approach. She went around it to the pigsty that stretched off the back of the cottage, closer to the trees and dragonberry bushes that edged the little valley where the village had been settled. The dragonberries attracted night fairies, and the traps kept them from stealing the eggs from the chicken coop.

Instead of opening the gate to get in, Maia hitched herself up over the low fence that surrounded the little sty. The three pigs inside grunted at her as she tucked herself into the shadows against the cottage's stone wall where the ground was dry and listened.

The guards slowed as they approached the yard. Maia could hear their footsteps better than their conversation, especially with her heart pounding so hard she felt she might be sick.

The villagers' chanting echoed against the hillside, their dramatic stomping as loud as their cries. "Witch! Witch!"

The guards checked the chicken coop, then they split up. One headed for the trees and the dragonberry bushes and the other stayed close to the cottage, peeking into the nooks and crannies around the woodpile and the night fairy trap. Maia caught glimpses of him as the pigs nervously paced their sty.

He was getting close. "Here, little witchy girl."

Maia glanced down at her skirt that covered her legs and

bare feet. It was a drab brown and blended into the shadows, but her shirt and the white of her hands seemed to glow in comparison. Then she looked at the hair that fell over her shoulder. It was a mix of blondes and browns, as if it couldn't make up its mind about what color it wanted to be, the lightest shade like streaks of sunshine and the darkest shade a honey amber. She scooped up handfuls of mud and smeared it over her hair and on her face, then caked it over the backs of her hands.

The guard came around the corner of the cottage and rested a hand on top of the sty fence. The pigs grunted a warning at him.

Maia held her breath. Two more steps and he would be at an angle where not even the mud and the shadows would keep her hidden if he looked her way. She closed her eyes for a moment, wishing on the grace of the hive fairies that he would keep walking.

"There you are," his voice was low but confident.

Maia's eyes snapped open. The guard leaned on the pigsty fence, a sinister grin on his face. She shot to her feet, the cottage wall at her back, and looked around at the yard, the chicken coop on one side and the trees on the other. She bolted to the side of the sty away from the guard, toward the trees, and swung her leg over the fence. The guard climbed into the sty from his side, startling the pigs. The animals panicked and charged, two toward the guard and one toward Maia. As she slid over the fence, it caught her forearm in its teeth and chomped down.

Maia screamed.

The pig released her. The second guard returned from the trees. He grabbed her shirt at the back of her neck and dragged her all the way over the fence. He planted her face-down on the ground, then he held her down with his hand on the back of her neck and his knee on her lower back. "Look, my Lord. I caught me a dirty little pig."

Maia grunted like the pigs, then sucked in a mouthful of dry dirt. She tried to blank out the pain from the pig bite, the pressure of the guard's knee, and tried to tuck her knees under her to stand. With every movement she made, the guard increased the pressure and more pain followed.

Footsteps plodded, shuffled, and high-stepped closer. Maia blinked at the sea of shoes that filled the seamstress's cottage yard. Blood dripped from her arm, soaking into the dirt.

At least the villagers had stopped their chanting.

Lord Graves crouched, his pantaloons spreading out above his buckled shoes and his tights. He peered down at her and smacked his scepter on her head. "You've been quite naughty, Maia. I took you into my home. Fed you. Gave you a place to sleep and a purpose to live. It's vexing the way you have repaid my kindness, poisoning my son's affections into thinking he was in love with you. That was a mistake that I promise you have only started to pay for."

He stood, kicking dirt into Maia's face. The guard who had been holding her down suddenly released her, then both guards gripped an arm apiece and hauled her to her feet. Maia blinked dirt out of her eyes, fresh tears washing more of it away. She looked at the crowd, silently pleading with each of them to say something, do something.

They all looked away.

At last, she met Tom's eyes. His expression now was pained, his brow pinched and his lips pursed together as if he were trying not to cry.

She had seen that expression before, on the first night he had kissed her. He had been telling her his favorite memory of his mother. The two of them were alone out beyond the kitchen

13

gardens, lying in a patch of soft grass and looking at the stars. Maia had reached out for his hand, and then he had propped himself up on his elbow, looked her in the eyes, and kissed her.

"To—" Maia began.

"Tom," Lord Graves cut her off, addressing his son but looking at her.

Maia never let her eyes waver from Tom's. She could see a war raging in his eyes, in the mottled flush in his face. Maybe…

"Tom, what do we do with witches? It is time for you to give the command. Go on, now. Hell is waiting." Lord Graves tucked his hand back into his belt again.

Tom opened his mouth, then closed it.

"Tom," Maia managed his full name this time, her voice trembling. "Please."

His hand lifted, as if he were reaching out for her. Then he blinked and it fell. He looked away from Maia, at his father and then at each of the two guards holding her.

"Take her to the dungeon."

2

THE HOUR GONE BY

Carving the little mark into the door of her cottage, Cerelia stepped back and looked at her handiwork in the fading twilight. The door was nearly covered in the neat little lines she had carved into the wood every full moon since she had lived here. She had never counted them. Maybe someday she would, but tonight was another full moon and she had things to do.

She loved full moon nights. In all the years she had been exiled to her garden in the middle of the enchanted woods, she had especially looked forward to these nights. Magical in their own right, these were the nights when her flowers and plants seemed happiest and most vibrant.

A tiny white spider climbed up her sleeve, sidling sideways like a crab until she sat happily on Cerelia's shoulder.

"Ah, my Xee. Are you ready for our full moon? I'm sure there will be plenty of night fairies for you to snack on. The dragonberries look ready to burst, and those nasty little pests won't be able to resist them." Cerelia looked at the spider sideways through the corner of her eye. "Maybe the reaper blossoms will catch a few night fairies, too."

The spider lifted a jointed leg and brushed it along Cerelia's cheek.

"Shall we?" Cerelia waited until Xee gave her an almost imperceptible nod, then she snatched up a basket and walked out the door.

The garden spread out in an irregular ripple of circles from where the cottage backed up to a ridge crowned with trees. A sectioned hedge several feet tall lined the perimeter, each section shaped like a giant flower petal with an arched opening in the center that looked out to the forest beyond.

Within the hedge, Cerelia's garden was the temperature of a late summer evening, full of green things of all shapes and sizes that twisted, bloomed, and spread out in a simple, winding labyrinth.

Beyond the hedge, the forest slept under a thick blanket of snow. Cerelia had grown the hedge from fox shrubs to remind her where the magical boundary of her garden was.

She could not leave and nothing mortal could enter, although she hadn't even seen a mortal creature in over a hundred years.

The cottage walls were made from the crumbling remains of the cabin that had been in the clearing when Cerelia had first escaped to this place, and thick vines that twisted through them. Cerelia had once made the vines bloom with little silver trumpet flowers, but the hive fairies had come first thing the next morning and picked them all. The noise of their wings alone had been enough to convince Cerelia never to cover her home in flowers again.

She did plant other things for the hive fairies, though. The dragonfruit trees bloomed with giant black-purple blossoms before they bore fruit, and the fairy bells tucked around the base of the dragonberry bushes swayed in the breeze like the bells they were named after.

Cerelia's favorite was the blooming honey clover that covered the paths of the garden labyrinth in a dense green blanket. The hive fairies could collect their nectar and Cerelia could watch them from her window without being awakened by their annoying buzzing at the crack of dawn. She even enjoyed watching Xee catch one of them now and then, although the spider clearly preferred the taste of the darker night fairies.

And Cerelia was certain the spider would get her fill of the little pests tonight. The full moon always brought them out in droves, and Cerelia had ripened a new crop of dragonberries all around her night fairy trap.

Cerelia was always changing the details of her garden, but some things she liked to keep in their places. The demon fruit trees, with their dark purple fruit full of juicy seeds, formed a pentacle with their connected roots, and the paths of honey clover defined the sacred shape of her garden labyrinth.

But sometimes she switched the bony roses with their jointed branches and tiny blooms with the reaper blossoms.

Reaper blossom flowers were her own invention as were many of the other things in her garden. They grew on stalks surrounded by long pointed leaves. The flowers looked like the heads of ravens with red beaks, and the beaks opened to snatch bugaboos or fairies when they flew too close.

Cerelia sat down on a soft mound of honey clover and set her basket on the ground next to her. This part of the garden also never changed. It was a small open space, ringed with toadstools and gnomeshrooms that seemed to take on the glow of the stars. This was where her heart was buried.

The moon rose above the treetops, bathing the garden in a silvery light. Cerelia raised her face to the round goddess in the sky, the single constant that helped her count some rhythm of time. She closed her eyes and listened to the quiet buzz of the first night fairies to collect around the dragonberries. She heard the rustle of a fae fox and a pair of kits slinking through the shrubs into the garden. Then she heard the soft snap of a reaper blossom as it caught a bugaboo.

She loved the sounds of her garden, but she loved most what gave it life. Beneath her, she could feel her heartbeat deep in the earth, pulsing up through every living thing within her hedge wall. The garden was her child now, springing up from where her own infant had been buried by the forest along with Cerelia's heart.

Cerelia looked around her garden, smiled, and sang a song to all the magical creatures within its walls.

> *Oh, my darlings, ripe and round.*
> *While the moon is full and the stars abound,*
> *Sharing your gifts of earth and sun*
> *Will blessed be for all and one.*

It was her own melody, the songs from her childhood forgotten over time.

Other things she had forgotten by choice, letting the forest have the memories she no longer wanted. She gave up the name of the boy she had once thought she'd loved, the one who left her at the mercy of her father and his guards as soon as she had discovered she was with child. She gave up the name of her father, too, but she still remembered the way his eyes had tightened in anger the last time she saw him and the way it had broken her heart.

She gave up everything that had been part of that world when she had been a mortal, that world that had betrayed her.

Xee scuttled down her shoulder, tickling the flesh of Cerelia's hand as the spider climbed down to the garden floor and disappeared from view between a pair of toadstools.

"Enjoy your hunting, Xee. I should have some demon fruit to gather, and maybe the goblin's cap gourds will be ripe." As Cerelia stood and picked up her basket, she got a sense of Xee's excitement.

The first time she had seen Xee had been on a night of a full moon. The strange spider had come to her garden to eat night fairies and beggar flies. Cerelia had picked a handful of dragonberries and the spider bit her. Ever since, Cerelia could sense Xee's thoughts like muffled dreams.

She made her rounds in the garden, starting with the goblin's cap gourds, dark red horn-shaped squashes that looked like they would wake the dead if someone put their lips to the ends and blew in them. Cerelia loved to boil them and mash them. They tasted like what she remembered of a mixed berry pie—sweet and tart. They grew in the shadows of the little cottage, their tendrils and giant club-shaped leaves curling out from the earth where the vines of the cottage walls grew up from the soil.

"Oh my darlings, ripe and round..." As Cerelia chanted, the gourd tendrils trembled, then wove through the air like a snake in a trance.

"While the moon is full and the stars abound..."

The tendrils lifted the squash to her. She thanked the plant for each one, praising how large it was and how deep the red. As she broke each one off at the stem, she felt the plant vibrate with the gratitude.

"Sharing your gifts of earth and sun will blessed be for all and one." She filled her basket half-full with gourds, glancing over at the dragonberry bushes that flanked the cottage. Cerelia had shaped them into domes with little hollows where the drunk night fairies could linger after they'd had their fill of the dark purple berries. From a point at the top of the domed top hung a night fairy trap, a metal cage that looked like it was originally meant for birds but with a much cleverer locking mechanism on the little door.

Tonight, Cerelia left the trap door open and unset. It would close after only a few had made their way inside and triggered the lock, and on a full moon night, it was easier to wait until the night fairies were all drunk on dragonberries and passed out in the branches and then collect them with Xee's help.

In the morning she would climb to the top of her cottage and trade them to the gargoyle for some eggs.

Cerelia approached the dragonberry bushes, watching a pair of fairies fight over a particularly large berry cluster. They screeched at each other, both grasping at the berries with clawed fingers. The fairies were hairless gray creatures with sharp teeth and sharp tempers. Their black and purple butterfly-shaped wings batted in fury until one of them tore its wing on a dragonberry thorn. That fairy fell to the ground while the other greedily took a giant bite out of the berry cluster.

Behind that fairy, Xee waited patiently. The spider had been there during the fight, her white body rippling as it grew to be the size of a house cat. While the fairy who had won the tiff over the berry cluster buried its face in the fruit, Xee crept behind it, reached out with her two front legs, and in a final flutter of wings, pulled the fairy into her jaws.

The berries fell and landed next to the fairy with the torn wing, who promptly snatched them up and gobbled them down.

Xee shimmied back into the branches of the dragonberry bushes to rest while she digested her food. Cerelia sensed her contentment and smiled.

Leaving the night fairies to the remainder of their drunken full moon indulgence, Cerelia headed to the fox shrub hedge that surrounded the garden. The shrubs had waxy green leaves shaped just like the fox's ears. While she had been in the center of the garden listening, she had heard a fae fox and kits hide in there, their black fur nearly invisible in the night. Cerelia set her basket down and approached with empty hands, crouching in her loose skirt as she searched in the leaves for the texture of their fur and the shine of their eyes.

She caught three pairs of eyes deep in the leaves, the mother's a luminous violet and the kits' eyes still a milky opaline shade.

Cerelia pulled a small piece of cooked gargoyle egg out of her bodice and reached out a hand. "Hello, little ones. How are my pretties this moon? Have you eaten up all the hoaxes? Scared away the rumples? Here you are. Come and get it."

She waited patiently, sitting as still as she could manage while the foxes sniffed at the egg. The mother took a step, then the kits bounded out of the bushes. One of them pushed the other out of the way, snatched up the piece of egg, and retreated back into the bush.

Standing, Cerelia watched them for a few more moments. She loved the little fae foxes, thinking of them as much a part of her garden as the plants she fed and tended. She was about to turn back toward the cottage where she was going to help encourage more blooms on her new reaper blossoms when, through the opening in that part of the hedge, she caught sight of a shadow in the trees that made her heart race.

A stag stood in the snow, its rack as wide as she was tall.

Cerelia stood frozen, watching the stag sniff the air. It was a proud creature, standing like a king in the snowdrifts.

Proud...and *mortal*.

THIS CURSED NIGHT

Everything hurt. Maia stretched her arms up to relieve some of the pressure on her wrists. The shackles had cut through her skin within the first few hours of being chained up in the dungeon below the Graves' manor.

Her head stung from where one of the villagers had pulled out her hair. Lord Graves had ordered the rest of her hair chopped off before they dragged her down to this lonely little cell. The butcher had reluctantly complied. It had given Maia a soft sliver of hope to see the pain on his face as he had sliced through each lock.

Slumped on the floor of the dungeon cell, she was covered in mud and the pig bite on her arm looked like it was already starting to fester.

Somewhere beyond the light of a single small torch, Maia could hear the drip of water. Her cell was dirty and damp and the skitter of rodents echoed along the stone floors. She was the only one in the dungeons...as far as she knew. At least she had not seen nor heard even the slightest sign of another person.

22

Maia's body hurt, but her soul felt like it was broken. She had been excited and proud to tell Tom that she carried his child. She had waited until she was sure, until her body showed it with the swell of her belly. Like a fool, she had believed every promise he had made to her. It hadn't been just his words, either. Tom had been so tender holding her in his arms, brushing his fingers through her hair as he told her about his dreams for the village once he grew up and claimed the title of Lord. He had promised he would have her by his side every day for the rest of his life.

Now each of those promises wedged their way inside like nails in rocks and sent cracks through her soul. Every moment she had spent with Tom, every tiny recollection, was tearing her apart.

Witch! Witch! Witch!

She wished she really was a witch. Right now, with her world ending, she wished she had the power to hex them all with the pox or send a swarm of night fairies to torment them with their tiny teeth and claws or take a hellhound as a familiar and send the beast to pull them from their beds and tear them to pieces one at a time.

Then they would truly be afraid of her.

But they weren't afraid of *her*. She was nothing but an orphan who had been raised by all of them. They knew her too well to ever be truly afraid of her.

No. They were afraid of the idea of her now, of what Lord Graves had told them she was. And they were afraid to go against that pompous caricature who waved his scepter around as if it meant something. They were afraid that their lord would send his guards to rob what little gold or jewelry they had, or even run them out of their homes and take their land.

"That fecking piece of rotting goblin guts," Maia muttered to the dungeon rats. "I would turn him into a pile of hoax guts and feed him nibble by nibble to the fae foxes. And his good-for-nothing offspring, too."

The babe stirred within her, like a flutter of fairy wings.

Maia knew that sensation should have been a joy. It was supposed to be the key to her happily-ever-after. Instead, it had become a curse. Because of it, she was chained to a dungeon wall while the villagers prepared to burn her alive as a witch.

She let her arms fall, ignoring the way the metal cut into the raw, bloody marks on her wrists.

Witch!

Maia wished she could erase it all. Somehow turn back time to the first day Tom kissed her.

She would slap him instead.

Somewhere in her exhaustion, she recalled a night at the midwife's when a girl from another village had been sent to theirs to deliver her baby. A shameful secret. The girl, then not much older than Maia's fifteen years, had been chanting over and over again in the delirium between her contractions.

> *Rumple, rumple, hear my plight.*
> *Come to me this curs-ed night.*
> *A bargain now I'll make with thee;*
> *Take my babe and set me free.*

At the time, Maia had been surprised by how angry the girl was at her unborn child, angry enough to call on the fearsome rumple goblins. But now she understood. It was a twisted feeling of betrayal. As if the angels in heaven had sold her soul to the damned.

The girl and her child had been missing the next morning, and no one—not her parents nor her lover—had come looking for her.

24

Maia had been an orphan since before she could walk. The entire village had become her family and now they wanted her to burn. If she couldn't count on them to protect her, a fairy tale chant was all she had left. She had seen night fairies and hoaxes and fae foxes—the creatures that lived at the edge of the woods and occasionally dared to venture out. She had never seen a rumple goblin, though. She only knew of them from the stories she had been told as a child to keep her out of the woods. There were more stories about the woods, stories about a three-headed witch who liked to eat human livers and her giant spider who lived there in the middle of an eternal winter.

And Maia believed them. All of them. Those tales were enough to keep even the grown men of the village from wandering inside those trees. The closest Maia had ever been was several feet from the edge of the enchanted trees where she was just able to see the drifts of snow.

What had once sounded dangerous held Maia's best promise.

"Rumple, rumple, hear my plight," she croaked out. Her throat was raw. She swallowed and started again. "Rumple, rumple, hear my plight. Come to me this curs-ed night. A bargain now I'll make with thee; take my babe and set me free."

A rat scurried over her feet. Maia jerked them closer and then struggled to her knees. She straightened as far up as she could and took a deep breath.

"Rumple! Rumple! Hear my plight!" She hoped Tom could hear her. "Come to me this curs-ed night! A bargain now I'll make with thee; take my babe and set me free!"

The final syllables echoed off the stones and the bars in the heavy wooden door of her little cell.

It felt good. She had wasted so many hours dreaming of revenge on Tom and Lord Graves that it felt good to do something other than wallow in dark hopes and soiled straw. She wanted Lord Graves to suffer, but Tom…he was the one who had truly betrayed her. He was the one who deserved the worst fate she could imagine.

She stood, the chains that held her to the wall too short to allow her to turn fully toward the door. She did her best, closing her eyes and sending her voice out through the barred window in the door and down the narrow dungeon passage. "Rumple! Rumple! Hear my plight! Come to me this curs-ed night! A bargain now I'll make with thee! Take my babe and Set! Me! Freeeeeeeee!"

Maia paused to catch her breath, sucking in a lungful of torch smoke and coughing it back out.

"Mortal, mortal," a scratchy, high-pitched voice began. "Here I be, come to hear your desperate plea."

Maia opened her eyes and gasped. A tiny, pinched-looking man with a red cap stood in front of her, the cell door behind him. Even though he was small, everything about him looked stretched, as if he had been tied to four pigs and drawn until he was twice the length and half the width he had been. Long bony arms and fingers tapped each other beneath a long, pointed nose. His pale skin stretched over delicate cheekbones and tall ears, and it sagged in folds down his throat.

"Blood for blood will end your plight; signed by soul this curs-ed night." The little man smiled.

"You're a—" Maia took it all in, trying to match the his appearance to the fairy tales in her memory.

"Rumple Six at your service." He offered a stilted bow.

"—goblin," Maia finished as she caught up to what he had said. "A rumple goblin."

"Yes. I am a rumple goblin. That was what you called for, was it not? You were not saying, 'Rumple, rumple' over and over again because you wanted a gargoyle to come grant your wish, eh, young lass?" The goblin dragged out the last two words, making the syllables as long as he was.

"No, I...I didn't know if you were actually real." Maia swallowed. "I remembered the words from another girl. I didn't know what it was. I was just thinking that... I...wanted..."

"You wanted to be free," the rumple stated simply. "You are desperate, alone, and facing a situation you imagine would have only existed in your nightmares. You can either take your chances with the mob outside waiting to lash you to a stake and burn you alive, or you can take your chances with a magic that you do not understand and that you cannot control. That is what makes you mortals both entertaining and easy to bargain with. You do not live long enough to truly understand the cost. My only advice is to bargain for something that will undoubtedly make it worth it. Blood for blood."

"Blood for blood," Maia repeated. Her mind racing with the one ending she wanted to this horrible day, a justice she thought she would burn before she ever saw it—Tom's body in shreds and Lord Graves tearing out his hair at the death of his precious son.

Maia wanted it so badly, to see Tom nothing but a steaming pile of muscle and bone, that she started to shake and had to wipe a line of drool onto her shoulder.

The rumple goblin stood patiently in front of her, waiting with his hands clasped at his waist and an expectant smirk on his face.

"Rumple Six, that was your name?" Maia asked. "What does the 'Six' stand for?"

"Indeed, it is my name, at least when I am dealing with humans." The goblin nodded. "Your kind loves to name things. The 'Six' is simply something you understand that has a vague relation to my goblin name. We discovered centuries ago that you do not nor cannot understand the true nature of anything magic, including the names of goblins."

"You seem rather excited to tell me about everything I don't understand." Maia narrowed her eyes at the goblin. "What about a witch? Would a witch be able to understand 'the true nature of anything magic'? Would she be making this bargain with you? Or would she send you off with a curse that made you especially tasty to gargoyles or dragons or something else with excessively large teeth?"

The goblin frowned. "You understand witches even less than you understand goblins. Witches are the only magical creature that is…created. A mortal turned immortal by the magic of sacrifice. I cannot say that I have ever met a particularly joyful witch. We goblins tend to leave them be, especially since they have no need for our particular vein of business. Now, to get back to this contract for which you called me—"

"Blood for blood," Maia nodded and swallowed.

Tom's voice echoed in her head. *Take her to the dungeon.*

She could practically taste her revenge. "Where do I sign?"

Rumple Six waved his wrist and instantly a scroll appeared in his long fingers. He snapped the parchment open. It was blank. "The contract. We will destroy one mortal of your choice in exchange for another mortal—that of your unborn babe."

As Maia started at the blank parchment, a golden line of fire swept across the page with a whirling flourish. It left behind a single verse in dark ink:

> *Mortal, mortal, here I be,*
> *come to hear your desperate plea.*
> *Blood for blood will end your plight;*
> *Signed by soul this curs-ed night.*

Rumple Six held it out while Maia read it in a whisper to herself. It was exactly the same verse the goblin had spoken when he had appeared in her dungeon cell.

"Blood for blood and all that, but what about setting me free?" Maia held up her shackled hands as far as she could on their short chain.

The goblin frowned. "Setting you free is not part of the contract."

"I'm not going to get very far if you don't help me get out of this dungeon. You remember that mob? The one waiting outside to lash me to a stake and burn me alive? If I'm going to get past them, I'll need to be able to sneak by, maybe even do a little running." Her body hurt at the thought of running. That was okay. Let it hurt. When this was all over, she would be alive and free of Tom and his unwanted bastard.

Clearly unhappy with the situation, Rumple Six's frown deepened to a scowl. He waved his free hand and the shackles fell from Maia's wrists.

"Thank you." She lightly rubbed the raw skin and stretched to her full height, facing the goblin directly. She held out a hand for a pen. "I'm ready to sign."

Now the goblin grinned, a greedy gleam in his eye. The parchment magically rolled back up and shifted into an entirely new shape. When the transformation was complete, a tiny tart sat on the goblin's palm. He held it up. "Sign by soul."

Maia blinked at the sweet. "So I...*eat* it?"

"Yes. It is our way to find you when the child is ready for us to take." Rumple Six ran his tongue along his lips.

"I thought you were going to take the child now." Maia shifted her weight uneasily, her glance passing from the goblin to the contract and back to the goblin. She wanted it all to end tonight, not months from now. This was not the bargain she thought she had asked for.

"The child is not ready. It is still unborn. We need a fully formed human infant, gifted by her mother, to grant us immunity to the night fairies. That is how the magic works. That is the contract." The goblin brought the tart closer to Maia with a step. "You should hurry. The one who betrayed you is coming."

Without another thought, Maia snatched up the tart and shoved it in her mouth. It was strawberry rhubarb, her favorite. As soon as she swallowed, a ball of heat simmered in her stomach. Then, in a quick flash, it flared through her entire body, finally lingering in her left arm. Maia looked down, and, just as the magic writing had appeared on the parchment, a flash of light scrolled a symbol into her flesh just below her wrist. It looked like a letter from an ancient language, twisting through and around itself in calligraphic lines. It burned for a moment, but the pain faded quickly.

"There, now you are properly marked. The contract is active." Rumple Six pressed his palms together. "There is… one final thing I would ask. A favor in exchange for setting you free."

Footsteps and voices echoed down the dungeon hall.

"What?" Maia's heart sped as the noise settled into a single set of footsteps that continued toward her cell door.

"I want to smell it." The goblin's dark eyes flashed.

"What?" Maia asked again, this time out of confusion.

"I want to smell the child before it's buried under the scent of the naughty boy's blood." He grinned, showing off a row of sharp teeth.

The footsteps stopped just outside the cell door, the glow of a torch highlighting the dungeon walls and the top of Tom's blonde head through the little barred window.

Maia nodded. "Hurry."

The goblin stepped close. The top of his pointed red cap came to Maia's breastbone, his long nose down by her belly.

Coming within a hair's breadth of touching her, he sucked in a deep breath.

"Yessssss." For less than a heartbeat, he stood there with his eyes closed and a look of euphoria on his face.

Then the iron bar on the cell door slid open with a scrape, and in a subtle shift of the air, the goblin disappeared.

Tom pushed the door aside and stepped inside her cell. The torchlight danced over his loose curls and burned like miniature flames in his eyes.

As angry as Maia was, she realized that what she wanted most, even after Tom's betrayal in the village square and her death now waiting down the hall, was for him to take her in his arms and tell her how much he loved her, how this was all a misunderstanding and he would speak to his father and the villagers and everything would be okay.

That he would tell them all the truth.

After all, he had come to her cell alone. That must mean there was something he wanted to say to her that he didn't want anyone else to hear.

Right?

Could she take it back? Could she tell the goblin that she had been wrong and had changed her mind?

"Tom…" Maia reached for him.

For a brief heartbeat, Tom's expression was one of pained longing. For a brief heartbeat, Maia thought he would steal a caress like he had done so many times over the past months when they had found themselves alone.

Tom took her hands, an expression of wonder and pity on his face. "It's because I love you, Maia, that I want you to go to the pyre with your head held high. The fire will release the darkness from you before you've had the chance to do any real harm. My father helped me see this. He helped me understand."

"No…" Maia hugged herself, as if that would protect her

against this madness that Lord Graves had planted in his son's soul. She pulled her hands from Tom's and stepped back until she was against the wall. The shackles, hanging from their chains, dug into the back of her leg. As she looked at Tom's eyes, at how the torch flame suddenly looked like hellfire instead of the light of love, all the hope she had just felt twisted in her gut and turned back into hurt and betrayal. She wished she could be even a small bit as fierce and determined with him as she had been with goblin.

Tom reached for her. "I'm here to take you to the town square. We have the pyre ready for you. Oh, Maia, how you will burn bright while we send your soul to hell where it belongs!"

Tears ran down Maia's face. She wanted to believe that this was not him, that this was Lord Graves standing before her and not the boy who was supposed to love her. She closed her eyes, wishing Tom would disappear.

"Rumple, rumple," she said softly. She heard a soft squelching sound and a heavy metal thump and flinched as warm liquid sprayed across her face and something sliced through her cheek. When she dared to open her eyes, she saw that the torch had been knocked off the wall and into the corner of her cell. It lit up a pile of dry straw.

Then she looked down in front of her at what was left of Tom. She only glanced long enough to note that his head was nowhere near the steaming pile of guts and bones on the floor. The fire spread through the straw in a quick blaze and licked at the blood pooling out from what was left of Tom.

The smell of it quickly filled the little cell. Maia choked on it, then held her breath as she stepped over the remains of her former lover and ran.

4

MORTAL, MORTAL

The stag stood for several breaths, air puffing from its nostrils into the cold night. The foxes jumped out of the garden and out into the snow, startled by Cerelia's reaction to seeing the unexpected animal.

She couldn't remember the last time she had seen a mortal animal. Everything in her garden had something to do with magic. Even the cottage had become a living twist of vines provided by whatever enchantment she had invoked the day she had begged the forest to protect her and her child.

Now, after countless years, something had changed.

The stag turned and bounded away, disappearing into the darker shadows of the trees.

Cerelia searched the moonlit landscape for any other creature that might portend a similar omen. Other than the night fairies passing out drunk on dragonberries and the reaper flowers snatching up bugaboos, even her little garden was relatively quiet for the night of a full moon.

Seeing the stag left her with a mix of unease and excitement. Cerelia tried to shake it off. She could puzzle through that while she drank her tea after the sun came up. Right now, she had things to do.

Cerelia picked up her basket and headed toward the cottage. It was time to get the night fairies gathered into the trap and tend to the rest of the plants in her garden. Once the gargoyle returned from her night's hunt and the fairies woke from their drunken slumber, she would set the night fairies free for the gargoyle to chase while she collected eggs from the nest on the cottage roof.

As she set the basket down on the cottage steps, she heard the crunch of footsteps on the snow. Had the stag returned? She turned to see something she would have expected less than a hive fairy at night. It was not the stag.

It was a *girl*. A *human girl*, stumbling through the snow toward her garden.

Cerelia froze, her mind trying to comprehend what she saw. A girl, about the same age as Cerelia had been when she had first come to the enchanted wood. She looked ragged and bloody, her bare feet in the snow the only part of her that wasn't smeared with soot or dirt or blood. The girl's hair had been chopped off in uneven sections, and her dress was torn in several places.

She was headed straight for one of the arched openings of the hedge.

"No, wait!" Cerelia ran to stop the girl from stepping over the stones that surrounded the garden. She didn't know what might happen to a mortal who crossed them.

"Help me," the girl begged, ignoring Cerelia's warning. She stumbled through the last of the snow. She held out her arms as she approached, and then she collapsed.

Cerelia caught the girl as she fell, a strange concussive sensation pulsing through her as the girl crushed a patch of gnomeshrooms. Fighting a surge of memories that had long lain dormant, Cerelia placed a hand on the ground and called up a thick vine from beneath the girl's limp body. It twisted around the girl's limbs and carried her to the cottage. Another tendril opened the door for the procession, the larger vine placing the girl gently onto Cerelia's bed and retreating back into the earth from whence it came.

Swatting away a nosy bugaboo, Cerelia brightened the orbs of light that hung from the vines inside the cottage and took a closer look at the girl.

She guessed the girl was about fifteen or sixteen, with long lashes and a gash on her left cheek. There was so much dirt and blood on the rest of her exposed flesh that Cerelia wondered how much of this girl she would be stitching back together.

And how in the goddess's green earth had someone so young—or at all—made it through the enchanted forest to Cerelia's cottage?

Xee, curious about the stranger, crawled in through the window and up the wall, still the size of a small cat. On the underbelly of her swollen white body, she had a dark red mark in the shape of a heart that Cerelia could only clearly make out when Xee grew to feed. The spider perched on a section of the vine walls near the upward curve of the thatched roof and watched.

The flames in the hearth burned steadily from a stone. Cerelia rarely needed a fire for warmth since the garden was in an endless summer, but she used it to cook and heat water. Setting a cauldron of water above the flames, she added a mixture of chamomile flowers and yarrow leaf to steep. She gathered some linen squares, a salve of dragon's blood and hive fairy honey wax, a spool of spider silk thread, a needle, a pair of scissors, a knife, and another bowl of clean, cold water.

As she settled herself next to the bed to get to work, the

fire blazed higher until the flames licked at the sides of the cauldron.

"Ah, my dear. Let's see what we have." Cerelia cut the girl's dress off in sections, trying only to save what still might be useful for some other purpose since the dress itself was too torn to count as clothing. Cerelia cringed as she guided the scissors through a couple sections that were so stiff with dried blood that the fabric cracked. She was relieved that beneath the soaked fabric, the girl mostly had some bruises and surface scratches that would heal on their own.

Her wrists were torn up pretty badly and the bottoms of her feet were raw from running on rough ground and hiking through the snow. Now that the body was stripped, Cerelia washed her with the cold water. The girl moaned and mumbled when Cerelia ran the rag over a particularly tender area, but she didn't wake.

Cerelia had to change the bowl of water twice before she had enough blood washed off to have a full assessment of the wounds. As she worked, she talked to herself and chanted, fighting against her own memories that flickered at the edge of her awareness like the fire beneath the cauldron.

"What have we here?" Cerelia inspected the girl's forearms more closely. One had a nasty bite that needed to be cleaned and, as the dirt and blood washed away from the other, Cerelia made out a faint burn scar in the shape of a vaguely familiar symbol.

"She's had quite a time of it, Xee. Looks like more than just shackles and a slap to the cheek with a knife," Cerelia spoke to the sleeping spider while she wrapped the girl's wrists with bandages soaked in her herbal concoction. Xee didn't seem to share Cerelia's concern over the girl, probably because the spider knew from the smell that most of the blood belonged to someone other than her.

And because Xee was quite contentedly full of night fairy.

Well, too bad for the spider. Cerelia had a job for her to do. For so long, she had been able to forget about the outside world, but now her own memories insisted that she find out as much as she could about what had happened to this girl.

And why the magic of her garden, which had kept the mortal world at bay for nearly a century, was starting to fail.

"Xee," Cerelia commanded, keeping her voice low in hopes that she wouldn't wake the girl who needed more than anything to sleep and heal. She felt somehow responsible and very protective of this mysterious person who had stumbled into her garden.

"Xee!" she hissed when the spider didn't even twitch a mandible.

Xee still lay contentedly on her little perch in the cottage's vine wall.

Cerelia pressed her hand to the wall and the vines responded, pushing Xee from her comfortable spot.

The spider dropped onto the bed next to the girl's head. She stretched up on her eight legs and shook herself awake, sending Cerelia a series of thoughts that very clearly conveyed how she felt.

"I know, you're full of night fairy and it's cold outside. Well, too bad, you lazy little exoskeleton." Cerelia ran a finger over the strange mark in the girl's arm. "I need to know what you can discover about this girl's situation. Something is happening to our garden and I have a feeling it has to do with her."

Xee sidled sideways off the edge of the bed and up through the window. Cerelia watched the spider's white body creep through the honey clover until she disappeared in the reaper blossoms and honey clover.

Cerelia returned to tending the girl. She threaded the needle with silk and stitched up the gash in the girl's cheek.

She bandaged her chewed arm with a poultice and rubbed salve over her raw wrists and scalp.

With a smaller pot that hung over the fire, Cerelia made herself a cup of tea and sat in a rocking chair, staring at the stranger sleeping in her bed.

Bruises, hair that looked like it had been thick and beautiful before it had been torn out and hacked off, the symbol burned into her arm…whatever had happened to her, it had been recent and harsh.

Over half the night was gone when Xee started to send Cerelia impressions of what she found at the edge of the enchanted trees.

The vine walls of the cottage with its little orb lights blurred into the background as Cerelia's attention was diverted to the space that existed between her and the spider.

The image through the eyes of a spider was multifaceted and slightly fuzzy. Torches and yelling. A crowd of men and women held pitchforks, lengths of thick rope, buckets of water, and chains. They argued with each other, their voices ripe with fear.

A man in the front of the crowd held up a lantern. He was flanked by two men in leather armor with faces twisted by scars. The man himself wore clothes that spoke of both overindulgent wealth and a lack of taste.

His voice seethed with entitled anger. "We have to find her. There will be no justice for my Tom until I have this little witch's heart on a stake in the town square and her soul is nothing but ash. I want to burn her piece by piece, taking her head last so she can watch the rest of her turn black in the flames."

The images coming from Xee dredged up memories from deep within Cerelia, moments she thought she had long forgotten. They layered themselves over the scene that Xee was seeing for her now.

"Take the babe to the woods and feed it to the gargoyles. No one need know this ever happened. I'll take Cerelia to the convent in the morning where she can take her vows and repent for what she has done. Perhaps the Lord can save her worthless soul." Her father's voice carried through the door. *"It will be like I never had a daughter."*

The sweat of labor beaded on Cerelia's brow, and she clutched at damp sheets as the baby tore itself from her body.

"Noooooooo!"

The villagers shifted nervously with their weapons.

"It's dark. We can't go in there now, Lord Graves. Not with the demons loose," said a man with a thick beard and a pitchfork.

"And the witch. I hear she's ten times more powerful when there's a full moon." A woman holding a bucket of water took a step back from the trees and the line of snow.

The pompous man holding the torch turned and snarled at them. "Cowards! All of you! If this had been about *your* son, *your* pride, *your* future, would you be such sniveling sacks of rotten meat out here ready to run from your own shadows?"

Cerelia cowered in the doorway, her newborn daughter hastily swaddled in the midwife's rags and held tightly to her chest. The wind cut through Cerelia's thin nightgown, and she trembled.

"We haven't found her, Captain, but surely she has not gone far," one of the guards said.

Her heart pounded. They were close.

"Release the hounds," *her father commanded.*

"The hounds? But, sir—" *the guard argued. There was a pause.*

Cerelia knew that feeling, the loss of words while meeting her father's angry eyes.

The guard continued, "She's still just a girl."

"Tell me, if this were someone who had taken your most prized *possession from you, would you be so lenient? She drowned my pride and joy in her sins," her father growled. "The hounds."*

Lord Graves signaled the two men who flanked him with a flick of his hand and they pulled out their swords. "Any of you willing to admit that you are too much of a coward to follow me into these woods, tell me now. I'll have you cut down now and save the world from feeding your worthless bones."

The woman with the bucket glanced at Lord Graves' two lackeys, then stepped forward. "After you, Lord Graves."

Another woman, older and lugging a thick rope, stepped up next to the first. "After you, Lord Graves."

Villager after villager joined them, their weapons ready.

Lord Graves nodded, clearly more satisfied with their response. He turned back toward the trees where Cerelia could see his face through Xee's eyes. Cerelia felt a slight sense of satisfaction at his expression of fear as he searched the shadows and the snow.

A hellhound howled and a gargoyle answered with its own cry.

The Lord Graves startled at the sound. He took a breath to compose himself before he turned back to face the villagers once more. "On further consideration, we will come back in the daylight when we can see her tracks. I believe we will be more successful in hunting the witch after we have a better plan. But I vow to you that we will find her and her unborn whelp, and we will have our revenge!"

The first hound found Cerelia in a blackberry bush outside the manor grounds. It sniffed and whined, not sure what to do. Cerelia pitied it, being sent to hunt someone who had been its friend since it was just a pup.

She reached out a hand. "It's okay. It's me, girl."

The hound whined again and licked her hand.

"There you go," Cerelia scratched the dog's ears, holding her

child in one arm. She needed to keep the dog quiet. She was losing too much blood to run far, and if she could pacify the hounds, she could find a place to hide in the village for a few days while she figured out what she was going to do. Maybe she could find the woodcutter's son and run away. He still didn't know that Cerelia had given birth to their child.

A guard yelled nearby and the hound backed up and growled at Cerelia.

More guards and more hounds.

Cerelia covered her baby with her arms and ducked her head, plowing through the thorny branches to the other side of the blackberry bush. She had a small head start as the guards and the dogs gathered around the blood she had left behind.

As the villagers left to follow the great Lord Graves to their homes, Xee scurried on her way back to the cottage.

The vines and walls came back into focus and Cerelia took a deep breath. She set down her tea, now cold, and hugged her arms around her shoulders. Tears ran down her cheeks, blurring her vision as she looked over at the girl, held together with bandages and stitches, sleeping on her bed.

When Cerelia had brought her inside, she hadn't considered how this girl might dredge up so many of her own ghosts. She had blissfully forgotten so much of that night, how it felt to have her heart beating *in* her chest in the moments when her father's cruel words broke it into pieces.

It will be like I never had a daughter.

As Xee crawled back in the window, the deep blue of the night faded to morning.

5

HERE I BE

Maia did not want to open her eyes. In fact, she didn't even want to be alive, or at least aware that she was alive.

Right now, being alive seemed to be more pain than it was worth. Her head hurt where her hair had been ripped out and her wrists stung beneath the pressure of the bandages that someone had wrapped over them. She had too many throbbing bruises to take inventory, and her cheek felt like it was going to split open again with every heartbeat.

But none of that was what had woken her. What had woken her was the flutter of the baby inside her, a reminder of why this had all happened to her in the first place. A movement that was getting stronger every day.

A thump prompted her to open her eyes. She looked up at a thatched roof that peaked at a point in the center, the thatch held up by a million twisting vines with little gray-green leaves. Round opalescent drops the size of acorns hung from the vines in a sea of translucent pearls.

Another soft thump shook the roof and a cloud of dust sparkled in the bright midmorning sunlight that streamed in through a window. The walls were almost completely covered in vines, these thicker than the vines that formed the ceiling, twisting in and out over the boards of the old cabin walls.

A pain shot down Maia's neck as she turned her head toward the window, trying to figure out exactly where she was. The light was too bright, forcing her to close her eyes again.

Where was she? She had a blurry memory of running through the snow, torchlight and the angry shouts of the villagers following her through the trees. She had tripped and fallen more than once, her hands and feet numbed by the cold. The gash in her cheek had left dark stains on the white snow.

She had been running for her life. She had run into the enchanted wood hoping that the villagers would be too frightened to follow her. Her relief at leaving them behind at the edge of the trees had been short lived, the terror of the creatures who haunted the woods at night had quickly replaced her terror of the witch hunt. A gargoyle had circled overhead, its wings spread in silhouette against the full moon, and she had almost fallen prey to the promises of a will o'wisp.

Then she had stumbled on the cottage. It looked so warm and safe, surrounded by a beautiful garden.

The witch's garden in the middle of the enchanted wood.

Witch!

"Oh, dragonberry drops," Maia muttered as she pushed herself up to a sitting position. Her head swam at first, then pounded. She pressed a hand to her head, cringing at her short, chopped locks. The blanket and sheet slipped down and she shivered despite a fire blazing in a giant hearth.

She was naked, bruises showing up in pink and purple over more than half of her.

43

Pulling a sheet out from under the blanket, Maia wrapped it around her and slid her feet to the floor. She searched frantically for her clothes, skimming over the three cauldrons of different sizes that hung in the flames of the hearth. There was a table with a stack of giant books, one of the tomes open and weighed down by a mortar and pestle. There were shelves with various jars like the kind Maia had seen at the village apothecary's, and a tea set on a tray next to a rocking chair. A few stacks of basic linen, a small metal tub, a hodgepodge of spoons and knives, a couple baskets...and finally a bloody pile of rags on the floor that looked like Maia's dress.

She snatched it up and inspected it, willing to wear it even with all the blood if it meant getting out of the witch's cottage. It had been cut open from the front, not any more useful than the sheet she already had on.

She stared for a moment at the blood, shivering as she recalled the sound Tom had made when the goblin tore him to shreds.

Oh, Maia, how you will burn bright while we send your soul to hell where it belongs!

There was another soft thump on the roof and Maia looked up, then back at the dress. A little white spider crawled sideways from the fabric to her hand.

Maia screamed and threw the entire pile of clothes onto the floor. She bolted out the door, the sheet tangling in her legs as she ran between a cluster of dragonberry bushes and a patch of flowers that looked like red ravens' beaks. She stumbled through a swarm of hive fairies, then she tripped on the twisted sheet and fell through the arched opening of the hedge. Half of her landed on the garden side and half of her on the forest side, and all of her hurt as if she'd fallen from a cliff.

"Running back to the torches and pitchforks, huh?" A

44

woman stood on the steep roof of the cottage, young, with long dark hair and basket in one hand. "In a sheet, nonetheless. You should try to look at least a little more presentable for when they burn you, or you'll make us all look bad."

Maia winced as she carefully got back to her feet. She shivered just outside the hedge wall, the breeze carrying the chill from the snow. She stepped back inside the garden, and immediately noticed the warmth and the sunshine

She looked up at the woman on the roof, pulling the sheet up off the ground. Was this woman the fearsome witch? She looked too friendly and...normal...to be a witch. "I wasn't going back to the pitchforks."

"Oh, no?" The woman crouched and placed a hand on the roof. A thick vine came up behind her, a night fairy trap dangling from the tip. It was a fancy one, but Maia still recognized it from the thick bar that slid down when it was triggered by the fairy wings. The woman smiled. "Where were you going? Out into the forest to live on snow and blackberries? I mean, I'm not saying you couldn't do it. It just sounds very cold."

Maia took a step back, waiting for two more heads to appear above the woman's shoulders.

Nothing happened.

As the vine with the night fairy trap swung over the woman's head, she reached up and grabbed it with one hand. The vine carried her off the roof until she dropped gently to the ground, and then it carried the night fairy trap over to a thicket of dragonberry bushes shaped into an arch and hung it there.

Maia continued watching in bewildered silence as the vine tucked itself back into the wall of the cottage.

That had definitely been magic.

Magic.

Witch! Witch!

The woman walked toward her, weaving her way through the patch of beak-shaped flowers. The strange blossoms moved as she stepped through, as if they were wishing they could follow her.

"You looked bad last night, and you look even worse today. I'm Cerelia." She paused for a moment, as if waiting for Maia to introduce herself.

Maia's eyes darted from Cerelia to the vines of the cottage walls and then to the flowers. Then she looked at the snow beyond the garden and down at the sheet she was wearing.

"You're a...the...witch in the woods." Maia hesitated, her mind still trying to catch up to the magic she had just witnessed. She fought the impulse to run, trying to puzzle through the contradiction of everything she'd heard about witches. The woman had obviously cared for her last night. If she were going to kill her, wouldn't she have done it already? Or left Maia out in the snow to freeze or be eaten by one of the gargoyles or hellhounds Maia was certain she had heard out in the woods as she had been running? "Are you going to eat me? Or turn me into a toad?"

"I was planning to cook you some breakfast." Cerelia motioned toward the cottage. "I promise not to turn you into a toad or eat you. Although I must say you've been very well tenderized."

Hugging the sheet tightly over her chest, Maia nodded hesitantly, still not sure she wanted to brave going inside even though Cerelia seemed quite pleasant for a witch who was supposed to have three heads and crave human livers. "There was a spider. On my clothes."

"Oh, Xee?" Cerelia glanced down at her own shoulder. The little white spider lifted its two front legs in greeting.

Maia had been so absorbed in watching the woman and

46

her strange garden that she had missed seeing the spider when Cerelia approached.

She backed up, her heel stepping back out into the cold. "Xee?"

Cerelia smiled. "I won't say she's harmless, but she prefers night fairies over pretty much everything else. And your clothes…well, they should probably be burned. Come on. I'll fry up a couple gargoyle eggs for breakfast."

A witch and her spider? Or a trek back through the snow to her fiery death at Lord Graves's hand?

Her stomach growled. Maia nodded even though she had never had gargoyle eggs.

Following Cerelia back inside the cottage, Maia stayed on what looked like an intentional path of some kind of flowering clover and as far away from the red flowers as she could, although she was certain they sniffed at her heels as she walked by.

The cottage was warm. As soon as they walked in, Maia was certain the flames jumped several inches even though Cerelia didn't add any wood or do anything other than set down her basket and stir the contents of the cauldron that hung in the middle. It was the largest of the three that hung from iron hooks in the hearth, the others stepping down in size like nesting pots. Steam rose from all of them, reminding Maia of a nursery rhyme about three bears and their porridge.

Cerelia glanced at Maia's bloody rags on the floor as she walked by them on her way over to a large trunk. She opened it and pulled out a dress. "Here. Blue seems like it might be your color."

Maia took the dress when Cerelia handed it to her along with a linen corset. The dress was a rich cornflower blue, the fabric plain but soft and certainly nicer than anything she'd ever worn in her life. She'd gotten herself into all this witch trouble in the first place thinking she was something special. She wouldn't make that mistake again. "This seems like it might be too nice for someone like me. I wouldn't want to ruin it. Perhaps something a little simpler? Or a little more worn?"

"Too nice for someone like you? What does that mean?" Cerelia straightened from where she had been digging in her garden basket. She held a pair of eggs, one in each hand. They were at least five times the size of a chicken egg, their shells a dark gray patterned with a web of lighter gray lines.

"I'm an orphan," Maia explained, feeling like that should have been enough for the other woman to understand.

Cerelia's shoulders fell a little and she pressed her lips together.

Pity? Maia didn't want her pity. She had always been a survivor, and she had lived a pretty good life for an orphan. She didn't want any pity, especially from a witch who lived alone in the woods.

Maia lifted her chin and stood a little taller, careful not to wince from how much it hurt to move. "I never went hungry and always had something to wear. The villagers took care of me well enough, each in their turn. I worked for them, and I worked hard. I always had a home."

"It looks like they took care of you, alright. Right up until they decided you should burn." Cerelia set the eggs down on the table next to the books and the mortar and pestle, then pulled a pan from a hook near the hearth. She crouched and slid the pan below the smallest cauldron and into the fire, resting it on a metal grate that spanned half the length of the hearth.

"Burn me? How do you know that? I haven't even told you my name." Maia lingered close to the cottage door, ready to run. "Did you see them? Did they come here?"

"They did not come here, but, yes, I saw them. Carrying

48

pitchforks and ropes and wearing fear and hate on their faces. Are those your beloved villagers?"

"That was only because of Lord Graves. I..." Maia wasn't sure how much she wanted Cerelia to know, although she had the feeling that this woman already knew far more than Maia even guessed. "He accused me of being a witch when I told him I was carrying his son's child. He threatened them and they had no choice."

Cerelia cracked the eggs into the pan. "Well, this Lord Graves certainly got the witch part wrong. Becoming a witch requires the kind of sacrifice you have not yet had the chance to make."

A sacrifice?

A shiver went down Maia's spine as she thought of the way Six had leaned close and smelled her baby.

Cerelia flipped the eggs. "You will be safe here with me if you wish to stay. There is magic in this garden to protect us from mortals if they even dare to venture into the woods." She looked up at Maia. "Although you are mortal and you are here."

Maia pressed the blue dress protectively over her stomach, hiding the faint lines of the rumple mark on her forearm.

Cerelia continued while she cooked. "I know the tales you all tell yourselves to frighten small children into obedience. They are not all truth, nor are they all lies."

Watching Cerelia tend the frying pan, Maia realized that the fire wasn't burning from stacks of wood. It was burning from large chunks of stone. She glanced around the cottage again, this time taking things in slowly. The bottles on the shelves were all labeled with strange names like "Dead Man's Bells" and "Duck's Food." The books had titles such as *Hecate's Cauldron* and *The Hidden Spells of Fairy Tales*, and a bubble popped on the surface of whatever dark gooey substance Cerelia had been grinding in the mortar and pestle.

There was definitely magic here.

Without looking away from where she cracked and cooked the eggs, Cerelia spoke over her shoulder. "You're welcome to wear the sheet if you'd like. It doesn't bother me. And as far as your Lord Graves and the villagers are concerned, they did not have to follow him. There is only one universal truth for all creatures, my dear girl, and it is that we always have a choice."

THE WITCH ALREADY IN THE WOODS

Cerelia pulled the smallest cauldron from its hook above the fire and poured the contents into a mug that had been carved from a large chunk of willow. She replaced the cauldron and settled in the rocking chair with the potion in her hands.

The girl had fallen asleep after she'd been up for only a couple of hours. She had eaten the gargoyle egg, although Cerelia guessed from the pinched look on her face she didn't like it. Then she had shared the skeleton of her tale with Cerelia, about Tom and the baby and how Lord Graves had accused her of being a witch. It wasn't until the end of that very brief story that she had even gotten around to telling Cerelia her name.

Maia was still wrapped in the sheet. Cerelia had tucked the blanket over her and moved a few leafing vine branches over the window to block the sunlight. The little cottage was dim, the magic vine orbs hanging from the ceiling at a half-glow. It had been enough light for Cerelia to find the spell she needed in one of the large books on the table. She didn't know how far her magic would travel. In all the years she had been here, she had never needed to find out.

"Did you see it, Xee?" Cerelia asked the spider after her witch familiar and only friend had settled on her hand. She had a habit of speaking her thoughts out loud to the spider even though the spider understood her thoughts more than her words. She spoke softly, careful not to disturb Maia. "Did you see the mark on her arm? She's made a deal with the rumple goblins. What is it the humans say? A deal with the devil? Well, after the rumples get a hold of her, she'll wish she had made a deal with their devil instead. Those goblins are a thousand times more dangerous than any of the devils I've heard of. No wonder she was about to try her luck on her own in the forest."

Xee rubbed her pincers together in agreement.

"There's no way this will end well, Xee, but we have to try. First, let's see what we can do about this Lord Graves." Cerelia sipped the potion. The liquid was thick and steaming hot, almost too hot to taste. It was like a thick cider sweetened with molasses. She smacked her lips and scrunched up her nose from the taste. "Night fairy wings."

The ingredient had come from one of the night fairies she had traded to the gargoyle, Septaria, that lived on the roof. Night fairy wings didn't exactly pluck off like insects' wings. Cerelia had to ask the gargoyle to snip them for her with her beak, the crunch making her cringe.

She needed them for this scrying potion and she was glad she had recalled the spell before the gargoyle had chomped the entire fairy down in one gulp.

"Look at her sleeping there. Do we all look so innocent when we close our eyes and let the hours pass in dreams? That cut on her cheek is already healing well. I'll clean it when we're done." Cerelia continued to sip her potion, feeling the heat and the magic settle in her stomach and spread slowly through her body. It was already working. "The trees are whispering to me, Xee. They're coming. That Lord Graves and his brainwashed villagers. Cowards, the lot of them. To do this to a young girl. An orphan that they raised. They all deserve to die just as they would have killed her. We'll keep her safe, Xee. As the forest has kept me safe all these years. We'll give her story a different ending than mine."

The potion tingled as it spread through her body, a warm buzzing that heightened her senses and made everything appear brighter. Everything in the forest was connected. The roots of the trees touched. Branches brushed each other in the wind. Deep beneath the ground, it was all fed by some ancient magic that Cerelia could sense but not name. For her, it had always been a kind but unforgiving magic.

And now the trees sent a message. Strangers had breached the enchanted boundary, carrying fire and hate.

Lord Graves.

Cerelia stood from the rocking chair and set her empty cup on the table by her spell books. She lifted her hand with the spider on it, meeting Xee's multi-faceted eyes. "It is time."

She stepped out into her garden and crouched down for Xee to hop from her hand to the ground. The spider scurried away through the honey clover, heading to where the witch hunting party had entered the woods.

Cerelia followed the winding path of her garden labyrinth, around the herbs and the demon fruit trees, to the center. She knelt down in the heart of the garden and placed her hands to the earth. The gnomeshrooms that grew between the fairy ring stones tipped toward her in greeting. The ground was cool and damp even though the dew had already dried in the morning sun.

Closing her eyes, Cerelia braced herself against the wave of energy and magic that sparked her nerves. She *became* the forest, ageless and vast. She became each fir tree down to the last needle on its branches, each fanning leaf of a fern, each twist of moss on the trunks, each stretch of root beneath the snow-crusted ground.

She found Lord Graves and his followers crossing a section of water-weathered stones left behind in a dry riverbed. They were at the border of the enchanted wood where the trees and snow met the sea and the warmer chill of spring.

With a deep breath, Cerelia focused her awareness back to the fairy ring, then guided the magic to where she had sensed the humans through her connection to the forest. Xee was ready to meet them, her white body now the size of a fae fox, blending into the snow except for the red heart beneath her belly.

The villagers wove their way through the trees, their boots crunching on the snow. It was a smaller band than the raging crowd that had chased Maia into the woods the night before, but they had taken the time to prepare and now they had twice as many weapons. Each man or woman had a rope hanging across his or her body, a pitchfork or blade in one hand and a bucket or torch in the other.

The Lord Graves himself led them, brave enough in the daylight to walk in front of his two scrappy guards. He wore plate armor that no longer fit over his gluttonous midsection and swatted at the ferns and branches with a sword that had started to rust.

"That little witch is in here somewhere. She will pay for what she did to my Tom. Burning is too generous a death for her. I will flay her alive myself. She will pay with pain and blood and eternal damnation." Lord Graves spoke to himself more than the villagers, his face twisted in a quiet but determined rage.

The images came to Cerelia as a dream in which the

edges were blurred, the sounds carried as vibrations through the leaves and trees.

The villagers' confident march slowed as the trees grew closer together. They split up as they wove their way in a loose group with Lord Graves in the lead.

"What if the other witch who was already in these woods ate her, Lord Graves?" one of the scrappy guards flanking him asked.

"Then we'll kill her, too, and send them both to hell where they belong," he answered without taking his eyes off the trees.

Xee climbed a tree above them, keeping Cerelia anchored to the location in the forest through their connection. The spider waited on a branch where the Lord Graves paused and scraped his blade on the bark.

Cerelia sent tendrils of magic down into the soil and little shoots poked up through the snow at the Lord Graves' boots.

The two guards stopped beside the lord, then the same one asked another question. "What if we can't find her before nightfall?"

This time Lord Graves stabbed the tree and dug the blade into the softer flesh of the trunk. "Then we'll burn her out."

The sword left a gash in the tree that Cerelia felt in her arm as if the lord had stood beside her and stabbed her directly. She sucked in a gasp and channeled the pain into the vines. They burst from the ground, their stalks growing as thick as one of Lord Graves's armored thighs. Weaving through the trees, they formed a wall ten feet high covered in finger-length thorns.

The Lord Graves stumbled back, tripping over a root that arched up as he came near. He landed on his rear, his face red and flustered. He pointed his sword at the vine wall. "Attack!"

The guards swung at the vines with their blades. Half the

villagers ran and half attacked in a panic. One man threw his torch instead of swinging his scythe and the woman next to him dumped her bucket of holy water on the flames. It went out in a sizzle and sent up a final wisp of smoke in surrender.

Another dropped his torch in the snow and ran full speed at the vines with his pitchfork, stabbing it into them so hard he couldn't pull the pitchfork back out. Xee dropped from her tree, tripling her size before she landed in front of him. The villager ran, but one of the lord's guards swung at the spider. Clamping her pincers on his arm, Xee cut it in half. The man fell to the ground, clutching his severed arm and screaming.

The Lord Graves regained his feet and came up behind the spider. He sliced his blade at the heart on her soft underbelly. A pearlescent substance oozed from the wound and Xee screeched in an otherworldly pitch. The spider spun around, pinning the lord to the vines with one of her forelegs.

Thorns shot through each of Lord Graves's shoulders, piercing through the back of his armor and out the front in sharp, bloody points. Another pierced the back of his left thigh.

Before Cerelia could send more thorns through his insides, his other guard waved Xee away with a torch and pulled the man down. Xee reared back, shrinking almost as rapidly as she had grown until she disappeared in a hollow in the snow.

The guard dragged the lord away from the vines, back to where only a few villagers remained. Two of them held torches and a couple of the others propped their lord across their shoulders.

"Burn it," Lord Graves commanded, twin trails of blood streaking the front of his breastplate. "Burn it all."

The villagers with torches stepped up to a tree and held the flames beneath the lowest branches.

"No," Cerelia begged in a whisper. There was nothing to hear her except the gnomeshrooms in her fairy ring.

The branches caught fire with a sizzle and a snap, and the villagers walked their torches over to another pair of trees.

Lord Graves grinned through his pain.

The help Cerelia had from the potion was waning. She pulled a little more power from the heart of her garden. The fight was not over yet.

Thorns shot from the vines. One pierced a villager in the head and his torch fell to the snow, but the tree he had been trying to light caught fire. Another thorn shot the remaining guard in the throat and another pierced Lord Graves's armor low on his right side. He jerked and grunted with the impact.

The remaining villagers fled, dragging their armored and bloody lord with them.

Cerelia remained in her fairy circle, feeding the vine wall to protect what she could while the flames grew and turned that swath of the enchanted forest along the dry riverbed to char. She knelt on the grass in her garden until the sun had set, working below the burnt surface to prepare new little trees and ferns to grow once the earth cooled. Although nothing like this had harmed the trees in the years she had been in her cottage, she knew the forest would heal itself.

That was the beautiful gift of growing things.

Finally, Cerelia released the magic and sat up inside her fairy ring. Twilight painted everything in shades of purple and gray, the dragonberries and the reaper blossoms almost black in the strange light.

She was stiff when she stood, her stomach twinging in sympathy to the gash that Xee had endured. She found the spider inside the cottage, nestled inside a bugaboo cocoon where she would sleep until she had healed.

Maia slept, too, although the look on the girl's face still revealed a lot of pain.

Cerelia brushed the girl's chopped hair back from her forehead and studied her in the soft glow of the vine orbs. So vulnerable. Cerelia wondered how anyone could accuse such a child of doing anything evil.

But Cerelia's own father had turned on her. It gave her a sharp pang of sympathy for this girl who had stumbled through her magic and into her garden. And there was a deeper emotion, something that Cerelia had cultivated in her garden but hadn't felt toward another person since the forest had taken her infant daughter. A fierce motherly love.

"I promise that I will keep you safe, Maia, whatever it takes."

7

SO THIS MAGIC MIGHT BE

"I wish I had magic like yours. I bet it makes this a lot easier." Maia swore under her breath and sucked blood from her fingertip. "Rotting fairy fodder. I didn't' know dragonberries had thorns. If I had magic, I would grow a thorn and poke it back."

The sun shone down on her shoulders and on her scalp where her hair had just started to grow back. Some part of her still tracked time as it was passing back in the village. The snow should be almost melted and the crocus making way for the daffodils and the tulips.

Cerelia walked over from where she was clipping herbs from the patches in which they grew out in the sections of the garden, her skirt kicking out in front of her.

Even though she had been with Cerelia for a month, Maia still struggled to believe the woman was over a hundred years old. She looked to be no more than Maia's age, with her long dark hair kept back in a thick braid and intense blue eyes that always seemed to be looking at something far away. It wasn't that Cerelia had directly admitted that she was that old. Maia had counted the full moon marks on the cottage door and figured it out herself.

The woman was *old*. And Maia believed it. She was certainly bossy enough.

"Dragonberries do not have thorns." Standing next to Maia, Cerelia parted the branches of the tall shrub. "They do sometimes hide nasty little surprises."

An angry little night fairy clung to a branch and hissed at them. Maia shuddered, looking at the night fairy's wrinkled gray skin. It reminded her of the rat that had run across her feet while she had been in Lord Graves's dungeon. She had to admit, though, that she'd always thought night fairy wings were a pretty mix of black and purple laced with silver.

"That wrinkled little bugger bit me!" Maia scowled at it and flicked at it with her fingers.

The fairy screeched and snapped at her.

Maia drew her hand back. "Maybe Xee would like to eat it for a mid-morning snack." She glanced around the garden for the spider. Currently the size of her hand, Xee was over by the reaper blossoms, fighting over a bugaboo with one of the dark blooms. The spider won, stuffing what looked like a giant orange ladybug into her mouth with her pincers.

"I think Xee is getting plenty to eat," Cerelia chuckled. "She certainly came out of that cocoon looking shiny and new. You have not yet seen her after she manages to catch a dreambeetle. She glows. Maybe she'll get one tonight during the full moon."

Maia watched the spider for a few more moments. Maybe she would just make sure Xee caught one so she could see her glow.

Xee had disappeared into some kind of cocoon for a few days after Maia had first stumbled into Cerelia's garden. The spider had been crawling around when Maia first woke in Cerelia's bed and then after she'd fallen asleep and woken up again, Xee was all wrapped up. Cerelia had offered no explanation and Maia had been too shy to ask. She had been busy nursing her own bruises and broken bones.

She brushed her fingers along the scar on her cheek. It was still fresh enough to be lumpy and ridged although it had healed cleanly. Maia had caught a glimpse of it in a little mirror that Cerelia had hidden in her trunk with her dresses. The scar was a dark pink line from her cheek to her jaw. At least it didn't hurt anymore.

She wished she could say the same for the memory.

Maia knew the scar would fade over time. If she had time. She looked at the faint rumple mark on her forearm, scrolled in some ancient calligraphy. Lord Graves was one kind of fear, but the rumples were quite another. And they would both be coming for her.

One for her soul. One for her baby.

She settled a hand over her rounding belly. The baby moved a little, the sensation still light and ticklish. She briefly wondered what it would feel like to hold it.

Shaking it off, Maia reminded herself that this baby had nearly gotten her killed. She had promised it to the rumples. Her freedom, her own life, mattered more than this mistake.

Right?

"The berries aren't going to pick themselves," Cerelia called to her. The witch stood in the middle of the goblin's cap gourds with a loaded basket hanging from her arm.

Maia sighed and parted some branches, looking for the night fairy before she dared to stick her hand in there again. "Why do we have to pick the dragonberries today? It's not like the night fairies can possibly eat them all in one night."

"Oh, they can," Cerelia replied. "Besides, I want the ripe ones for dragonberry wine. We should celebrate."

Searching for the berries that had turned a shade of red so dark they were almost black, Maia plucked a couple and

61

dropped them in her bucket. "Celebrate what? Pulling weeds and being bit by a night fairy?"

Cerelia chuckled. "No, dear girl. Celebrate being alive. It's a full moon tonight and we have a lot more to do. The night fairies will be out in droves, and they are always voraciously hungry."

"What about normal berries like strawberries and blackberries? Why don't the night fairies eat those?" Maia plucked a handful of dragonberries and dropped them in her basket.

"Ah, strawberries," Cerelia sighed, a wistful expression on her face. "I haven't had strawberries since I've been in my garden. They don't grow here, and I think it has something to do with the magic that protects this garden and why it's always warm within the boundary of the hedges."

"Strawberries can't grow in here?" Maia looked at the plants in the garden. Many of them were strange plants that she knew Cerelia had created, but there were also herbs that many of the villagers had grown at home. "Maybe one of your giant books could help you figure out how to grow magical strawberries."

Cerelia laughed. "Xee collected those grimoires for me over these long years, sometimes traveling for months to find them and bring them to me. I have not yet found a spell for strawberries."

"Then make a wish," Maia shrugged. A wish seemed significantly less complicated than a spell.

Maia looked around the garden. She spotted a bugaboo hovering near the reaper blossoms. She set her basket down and rushed to catch it before one of the blossoms caught it. It was bigger than she expected, several times the size of a fat bumblebee, and it squirmed against her palms. She brought it to Cerelia, careful to stay on the paths of honey clover.

She cracked her hands open wide enough to see the

bugaboo inside, but not so wide that the creature could escape. "Here. Just whisper what you want and set it free, and your wish will come true."

Cerelia set her basket down and carefully took the bugaboo from Maia. "Aren't you too old to believe in bugaboo wishes?"

Maia smiled at the idea that maybe she had a little magic of her own. "Aren't you too old not to?"

Cerelia stared at her for a moment, some emotion Maia couldn't identify flashing through her eyes. Then she brought the bugaboo up to her face and whispered. "I wish for a basket full of fat, ripe strawberries."

The bugaboo buzzed away as soon as Cerelia opened her hands.

"See?" Maia asked, quite pleased with herself. "What good is being a witch if you forget about ordinary magic like making wishes?"

Cerelia smiled. "I suppose you're right, my girl."

"I know I'm right." Maia returned to the dragonberry bushes. "Can't you just use your magic to make more? Or make them ripen as you wish? I bet you could even turn them directly into wine without having to do this annoying, tedious part."

She reached in for more berries, then snatched her hand back when the night fairy hissed. Damn little bugger.

Maia had to admit, though, that she had instantly fallen in love with the flower petal-shaped hedges that surrounded the garden and the constant fluttering of the hive fairies' golden wings as they collected nectar from the blooming honey clover and the dragonfruit blossoms.

She would put up with the night fairies if it meant she could have the rest of it.

"I could ripen them, but I don't know how to turn them directly into wine," Cerelia admitted.

Maia watched as the witch magicked a gourd into her basket, then caressed the leaves as if she were petting a cat.

Cerelia continued. "Magic like mine is like speaking a language made of vibrations and sensations rather than words. Although words have a lot of power in them, too. I prefer to ask the plants to do what I wish rather than forcing them to. When the fruit ripens on its own, that is the plant's gift to us. In return, we give the plants the greatest gift of all —love."

A sharp little pain jabbed in Maia's heart. She knew enough about love to know that it was more cruelty and heartache than the beauty and grace that Cerelia gave to her garden. All of the villagers had cared for her and had still chanted for her to burn.

And Tom. His betrayal cut the deepest, professing to love her at the same moment he begged her to go willingly to her own death.

She left the night fairy alone and moved to a different part of the dragonberry bush to collect her berries. "I've had more of love than I care to ever have again. Love is nothing but lies. It's exactly how I ended up beaten and nearly ended up burned to death."

And pregnant.

Maia paused and watched as Cerelia lifted her hand up to her eyes. The spider was perched on the back of her hand, fat with the bugaboo. Xee brushed Cerelia's nose with her two front spider legs.

"I was like you once, Maia. What I thought was love drove me into these woods, nipping at my heels. These woods saved me and kept me safe." Cerelia smiled affectionately at her spider. "When we care for things, we grow to love them. It is one of the most ancient rules of our existence. You'll know that without a doubt when you hold your baby in your arms."

As Maia turned her focus back to the berries, a thread of guilt wound its way through her heart. Cerelia had been caring for Maia as if she had been Cerelia's own child, but what would Cerelia do if she knew about the rumples? Would she still care for Maia like she cared for her goblin's cap gourds?

Maia would tell her, but not yet. She liked it here in this magical garden with its nasty little night fairies and strange plants. She liked the way Cerelia told her fairy tales at night as they sat in front of the fire like Maia's mother had done before she died.

She would tell Cerelia…but not yet.

Cerelia came over with Xee still on her hand and her basket swinging heavily on her arm. She reached for Xee to climb from her hand to the dragonberry bush. The spider disappeared into the thick clusters of berries and waxy dark green leaves.

Maia gave Cerelia an uneasy smile.

The woman brushed Maia's hair back from her face. "Give it time, Maia. The pain is already fading. Your bruises have cleared up and the cut on your cheek is healing. Your heart will, too."

Maia shook the short auburn curls that had started to grow out from her chopped off hair. "Give me a few more months and you won't even be able to tell that I was nearly beaten to death by the villagers who raised me and chained me up in a dungeon while my unborn child's father tried to convince me to willingly be burned alive."

Cerelia gave her a tight smile and played with a curl. "Your hair is growing back beautifully."

The gesture dredged up a distant memory. Maia looked away from Cerelia's gaze, uneasy with the affection.

"When I was little, my other used to sit me beside her while she mended clothes for the villagers and tell me fairy tales of princesses. My favorite story was about a princess locked in a tower by her evil *gothel*. The princess grew her hair twenty ells long. She would let it down out of her window and that's how the prince climbed up to see her at night. I used to put a scrap of cloth on my head and pretend my hair was that long and my prince was coming."

"Gothel?" Cerelia asked.

Maia turned to her and smiled shyly. "It means 'godmother' in my village."

Cerelia nodded. "Godmother."

"After my mother died, all the women in the village took turns caring for me, but none of them officially took me in. I never had a true gothel." Maia studied Cerelia, wondering what the woman was thinking as her eyes turned toward the trees in the distance and a wistful expression settled on her face. Maia turned back to the dragonberry bush. She didn't really want to talk about love and all that. She'd rather be bit by the nasty little night fairy again. "Still, if I had magic like yours, I would move these dragonberries near your hedge and put the reaper flowers here to catch all the pests that nibble on your herbs."

The gargoyle on the cottage roof opened one eye at the mention of hive fairies. Then she took a deep breath and closed it again.

"Oh? Quite a list. And what else would you do with the magic?" Cerelia raised an eyebrow, a mischievous look on her face.

Maia plucked a handful of dragonberries and dropped them in her bucket. "I would use it to ripen the berries and make them fall into the bucket all at once without having to pluck them one at a time."

"Well, I might be able to manage some of that. Watch." Cerelia handed Maia her basket of herbs and gourds and wove her way along the path of honey clover, collecting a blossom or a leaf from each of the plants.

Once Cerelia had her hands full, she stepped inside the fairy ring in the center of the garden and laid out her little harvest in a neat half-circle. Cerelia knelt with her hands pressed to the ground and chanted.

> *Blessed be by the law of three,*
> *I gave my heart so this magic might be:*
> *One beat for yesterday, the hour gone by;*
> *One beat for today when the hour is nigh;*
> *One beat for tomorrow with hours unknown.*
> *The essence of one becomes the essence of another;*
> *Where the spirit goes, the flesh must follow.*

Maia took a step back as the ground began to tremble. Then the fairy bells changed right before Maia's eyes. The short, delicate stalks with gray-green leaves extended into the scrolling darker green fuzzy stalks and scalloped leaves of the basil. The transformation finished with a burst of blue bell-shaped blossoms at the end of each stalk and the shrubs popped beneath one of the demon fruit trees.

Cerelia continued to chant, "Blessed be by the law of three, I gave my heart so this magic may be…"

Next to Maia, the dragonberry bushes shook and then shimmered. Maia took a step back and watched as the berries darkened and fell into small heaps onto the honey clover below. The night fairy plopped onto the ground with the berries and shook its head. Disoriented, it flew in an uneven path toward the reaper blossoms. One of the beak-shaped leaves snapped at it. The fairy screeched and fluttered back toward the dragonberry bushes in a drunken panic.

The trembling stopped and Cerelia stood in the fairy ring. The blossoms that she had set out on the ground were gone. She smiled. "It was certainly time for some redecorating."

Maia looked with amazement at the fairy bells and the flowering basil in their new locations.

"You still have to collect the dragonberries. We only take what is ripened and gifted to us." With that statement, Cerelia certainly sounded much older than she looked.

Maia didn't even care about having to pick up the dragonberries. She would work all day if it meant she could witness such beautiful things. "Yes, magic like *that*!"

Cerelia's expression darkened as she crouched in the middle of the fairy ring and brushed the grass that grew taller over the very center. "I told you, Maia. Magic like mine takes a great sacrifice. 'A witch is born when from her is torn something greater than her soul.' I pray you never have to pay that price."

Maia only nodded, not sure what to say. Her hand hovered over the rumple mark on her arm.

Signed by soul.

8

THE ESSENCE OF ONE

Cerelia smiled at the moonlight flooding in through the cottage window. She was excited to show Maia the garden under that holy light. After Maia had shown her complete fascination with everything in the garden, Cerelia had worked through the afternoon to prepare a surprise for the girl. Her magic flowed strongest under the full moon, and it had been tugging at her for the past few days as it waxed full.

"Can we go out now?" Maia looked at Cerelia, her eyes bright despite the shadows in the cottage. Still, there was an underlying sense of distrust coming from the girl.

"In a moment. Not quite yet," Cerelia shook her head. The moon was almost at its peak above the enchanted forest. She picked up a strip of linen that she had cut from one of her bolts of fabric. "Close your eyes."

Maia frowned, uneasy.

"I promise it will be okay. I told you, you are safe here." Cerelia tried to soothe her.

After taking a deep breath, Maia nodded and closed her eyes.

Cerelia tied the linen behind the girl's head, feeling some sympathy for the girl's discomfort at being blindfolded. It had already been a month. She wondered briefly how long it would take before Maia trusted her.

Hooking her hand in Maia's elbow, Cerelia walked her slowly toward the door. "We're past the rocking chair. Trust me." Cerelia reached forward and opened the door. Xee scurried out and the night air blew in gently, smelling of a mix of pollens and the snow and evergreens beyond the fox shrub hedge. "Now, a small step over the threshold."

Maia scuffled forward in small steps, feeling her way with her bare feet. "Through the door that says you're a hundred years old?"

"A hundred years?" Cerelia paused, surprised. She had never counted the marks on the door. It had been a way to mark the time, but time had grown to have less and less meaning to her.

Until Maia had stumbled into her garden.

Maia stepped through the doorway and out onto the wide flat stones of the garden path. "Probably closer to one hundred and twelve, give or take. I'm not quite sure how full moons translate to years, but I think I came close."

One hundred and twelve. Cerelia shook her head. What did that matter when she couldn't leave her garden, anyway?

Then she completely forgot about moons and months. She froze, Maia halting beside her.

In the center of the fairy ring, right above where her heart was buried, there was a rabbit. A plain rabbit, its gray fur turned silver by the moonlight, nibbling on tall green shoots that hadn't been there when she and Maia had returned to the cottage at sunset.

"Are we there? Can I take the blindfold off?" Maia asked, turning her head as if she could look around.

"Not yet," Cerelia answered quietly. The rabbit lifted its head, long ears standing tall, and sniffed the air.

"What's wrong?" Maia asked in a low whisper.

Cerelia realized she had tightened her grip on Maia's arm. She relaxed her hand. "Nothing. I just remembered there was one little thing I still needed to do for your surprise."

The rabbit scampered away through the fox shrubs and disappeared into the snow and trees beyond the garden.

Cerelia led Maia the final short distance and settled her in the center of the fairy ring. "Okay, don't take off the blindfold yet."

"Okay," Maia nodded, her arms hugging her chest when Cerelia released her grip. "I already have goose pimples. And I'm really hoping the surprise isn't something like a pet night fairy. I'd rather try to hatch one of those gargoyle eggs."

Despite her worry over the rabbit, Cerelia smiled at the girl's response. Maia was proving to have quite a sassy streak.

The witch crouched to the earth and plucked a thin green stalk from the ground. Something about it was familiar, as if she had seen it somewhere before, a long time ago. She tucked it in her apron and knelt with her hands on the ground. She closed her eyes, feeling the pulse of her heart deep in the earth below her, her connection to the forest complete. Seeking the thousands of tiny seeds she had created earlier that day, she sent out a thread of magic, a vibration that spoke to the growing things. Answering the vibration, the seeds woke and cracked open. Tiny seedlings grew up and pierced the soil, seeking the night air. Their leaves stretched open, then a blossom grew up out of the center of the stalk and bloomed. Petals spread open and turned down like a parasol. They drank in the moonlight and glowed like the vine orbs inside the cottage.

Cerelia sent one final surge of magic through the garden and the blossoms broke free from their stalks. She opened her eyes and stood next to Maia. The forest breeze caught the blooms and they floated into the air above the garden like a glowing sea of stars. Cerelia reached out and touched one that floated at the height of her waist. It twirled like a dancer, the white inside the petals flowing like pearlescent milk.

"Now." She untied Maia's blindfold, her heart swelling at the look of awe and wonder on the girl's face.

"They're...beautiful. They look like little pearls that became stars." Maia followed one out of the fairy ring and plucked it out of the air. "It's a flower!"

Cerelia also picked one out of the air. "I call them the Tears of Midnight."

Maia looked at her, a frown suddenly tugging at the corners of her mouth. "You mean, like the moon is crying?"

The contrast between the beautiful flowers and Maia's frown was enough to make Cerelia laugh. "Oh, child. Not all tears are from sadness and pain. We can also shed tears of joy, Maia. Even when it feels like our darkest hour." She tucked a flower in Maia's short curls.

Maia smiled. "You're very wise for someone who's only a hundred and twelve years old."

Cerelia returned the smile. A hundred and twelve years old sounded ancient, but Cerelia was just beginning to feel alive. The girl gave her a sense of hope that she may someday have a life beyond the hedge. "I have learned it all from the trees and the ferns and the roots of the earth that are much, much older than any of us. The wild things have a lot to teach us if we take the time to listen."

Maia looked around at the flowers that floated in the breeze like an intimate sea of stars. "Do you think they'll speak to me?"

"Of course, but that is not the question," Cerelia said.

Maia looked at her with a curious expression.

"The question is whether you are ready to listen," Cerelia

explained. She enjoyed how eager Maia was to experience everything. It gave the whole garden a more vibrant existence.

Before Maia could respond, a screeching came from the dragonberry bushes. A pair of night fairies fought over a cluster of berries. One took a swipe at the other's wing and they both fell to the ground.

Cerelia sighed.

"I don't think the night fairies listen to anything other than their greedy stomachs," Maia said.

Pulling the green stalk from her apron, Cerelia ran the length of it through her fingers. "Oh! While they're fighting over the dragonberries, we should be drinking our wine. I'll fetch it from the cottage."

Maia nodded, her attention completely focused on the Tears of Midnight. She stepped out of the fairy ring stones and toadstools that surrounded the heart of the garden and reached for the glowing blossoms that spun and bobbed over the reaper blossoms and the fairy bells and the goblin's cap gourds. A few had floated out of the garden and were almost to the trees that surrounded Cerelia's clearing.

Once inside the cottage, Cerelia turned up the light of the vine orbs and looked more closely at the stalk she had plucked from the garden's heart, even though she could feel its shape just as well in the dark as she could see it in the light.

Most of all, she could feel that it wasn't magic. And neither was the rabbit that had been eating it.

Just like Maia, they had crossed the boundary into her garden.

Quickly, Cerelia flipped through a couple of illustrated herb encyclopedias that Xee had brought back from one of her many foraging trips over the last century. Cerelia vaguely recalled that these particular references had been abandoned at a tower near the sea. Cerelia didn't exactly know where, she just had some sense that it wasn't far from her garden.

"There it is. Rampion." Her finger ran along an illustrated page. The stalk in her hand matched the drawing. "A regular old onion growing right in the middle of my garden, Xee."

"Cerelia! Come see this!" Maia called to her. "It's amazing!"

Setting the stalk between the pages to mark the spot, Cerelia closed the book and hurried over to a pair of pitchers full of dragonberry concoctions. She poured a glass of juice for Maia and a glass of wine for herself and, turning off the vine orbs with a flick of her wrist, returned to the garden.

Maia spun in a circle in the middle of the reaper blossoms, her arms spread wide and her skirt flaring out. Around her, the Tears of Midnight spun with her, caught in the whirl.

After a moment, Maia paused. She stumbled a little before falling to her knees. "Whoa! I'm dizzy. But wasn't that amazing? It's like being in a waterfall made of moonlight."

The grin on the girl's face was contagious. Despite the unease from the rabbit and the rampion, Cerelia's heart flooded with joy. Maia was genuinely happy. At least at this moment, it seemed that she had started to leave Tom's betrayal and the bloodlust of the villagers behind her.

Cerelia wondered if her own daughter would have looked anything like Maia. She couldn't remember what her child's father had looked like. She had forgotten him very purposefully, and the pain of missing him had quickly been soothed by the flowers and the vines and the other magical plants she nurtured and tended. And she had also learned very quickly that in exchange for the forest's protection, she could never leave the garden where her heart was buried. Nothing mortal could ever enter and she could never leave.

But the rabbit...

Sipping her wine, Cerelia left Maia in the middle of the fairy bells, the girl completely fascinated by the glowing Tears of Midnight, a fascination that belied how innocent she still was.

Cerelia made her way carefully through the labyrinth to the hedge. Standing beneath an archway, she stared at the forest beyond for a long moment, studying the way the moonlight emphasized the dips and hollows of the snow. She remembered helping the fox shrubs grow tall to remind her where the magical boundary was. She had only crossed it once before she had clearly understood what it had meant to give her heart and her child to the magic of the forest. Her chest had seized up and she couldn't breathe. She didn't know how close she had been to death at that moment when she had managed to crawl back into the garden like an animated corpse. She had gone out of her way to avoid repeating that experience.

The snow that had once covered the ground right up to the stones had melted back by almost a foot. The same thing had happened along the edge of the trees where Lord Graves and his villagers had burned it. Cerelia had been working every day to heal that swath of torched trees and undergrowth since the last full moon. The green living things were making a comeback, but the snow had not returned. And, Cerelia suspected, it was melting even further into the trees just like it was melting everywhere as spring replaced the winter.

The magic had definitely shifted, but how far?

Cerelia took another sip of her wine. "Maybe…"

She took a small step, her toe lined up with the last hedge leaf. It felt strange to be standing on the line that had always divided her beautiful life of magic and eternal summer from death. Even the moonlight seemed to shine down on the garden side of the wall more brightly than on the snow that surrounded it.

Taking a deep breath, Cerelia held it while she slowly extended her arm beyond the boundary.

As her hand passed through the invisible barrier that defined her garden, the flesh appeared torn and rotten, her finger bones showing through where the skin and tissue had rotted so badly that it had fallen away.

Snatching her hand back, Cerelia stepped back into the safety of her garden. She released the breath she had been holding and stared out at the trees where she had first seen the deer.

She was not free...yet.

9

A THOUSAND LIVES

The early morning light was thin and silvery, a little like the Tears of Midnight that Cerelia had surprised Maia with a month before. It was becoming Maia's favorite time of day, when there was enough light to show the beauty of everything without the flaws, as if the world had been painted perfectly.

Maia glanced again at Cerelia to make sure the witch was still sleeping off the previous night's full moon. The woman looked even younger with her eyes closed, her face surrounded by her dark hair. Maia couldn't believe that she was over a hundred years old.

She slid off the bed and fished a pair of makeshift leather boots out from under the mattress along with one of Cerelia's old cloaks that she had found in the trunk. She dumped it in a gathering basket and tiptoed out the door. The garden was already the temperature of midmorning in summer, most of the plants still sleeping like their mistress.

A couple drunk night fairies snored on the grass beneath the dragonberries, and Septaria watched Maia from the roof with a single sleepy eye.

Cerelia had allowed Maia to climb up and feed the gargoyle after the last full moon. With the help of Cerelia's vines, Maia had made her way up the slope of the thatch and had released the fairies.

The gargoyle had spread her wings and snatched up a dozen fairies in a matter of minutes.

But what Maia remembered most from that day was the view of the garden from the roof. Cerelia's labyrinth was in the shape of a flower, with the dragonberries flanking the cabin in the shape of giant leaves and the honey clover paths drawing layers of flower petals that radiated out from the center. Five demon fruit trees grew in even spacing around the center, each labyrinth petal beyond that filled with herbs, gourd vines, fairy bells, reaper blossoms and other plants in ripples of color and texture.

Maia felt, in that moment, as if she were seeing Cerelia's soul.

In return for that, and the spectacular Tears of Midnight, Maia had been planning a surprise.

Xee led the way through the grass, her tiny white body flickering when it caught the morning light. Maia hoped that Xee hadn't given the surprise away to Cerelia. She still wasn't entirely sure how the two of them communicated, but she only needed a few hours to collect the strawberries and return. She had waited until Cerelia was on the roof with the gargoyle to ask the spider to help her find the strawberries.

Apparently, Xee had agreed.

Maia stepped through the hedge and sat down to put the boots on. She had fashioned them from an old leather vest from one of Xee's long ago foraging adventures. Cerelia had been cutting it into strips for ties. The ground on the outside of the hedge was much colder than it was on the garden side, but it was no longer frozen. Cerelia spoke only a little of the change in the forest with the snow melting, but

Maia could tell that the woman was both anxious and excited for it.

As for Maia, she had been happily devouring the rampion that had sprung up in the center of the garden. It seemed as if the baby inside her couldn't get enough.

Maia stood and took a couple steps to test the leather tied over her feet.

"I will never understand why that woman has insisted on wearing these long, archaic skirts for the past century instead of fashioning even a single, decent pair of pants. I had to wear a dress at Lord Graves's manor. It was a tight, stupid thing and I don't miss it at all." That dress had been the one that had turned into the crusted pile of rags after Cerelia cut it off her. Good riddance. "You know, if I had been stuck in the woods, alone, in a magical garden where it is always summer, I wouldn't worry about pants. I wouldn't wear clothes at all. I'd let the sun shine over every inch of me and swing from those vines. I'd be as wild as the trees and the rampion that sprung up in the middle of the garden."

She looked down at her growing belly. "On the other hand, I have no choice, do I, Xee? A skirt it is for now. And a cloak for the snow."

The baby kicked as if on cue and Maia exhaled, reluctantly admitting to herself that she was proud that the baby was strong.

The spider's only answer to Maia's monologue was to crawl straight into the trees.

"Alright, here we go. Now let's go find those strawberries." Maia adjusted the cloak and traipsed along behind the spider. She had to concentrate to keep the spider in view while paying close attention to where she was stepping. The thin leather of the makeshift shoes did little to protect the soft undersides of her feet from the occasional stone or knobby root, but tender feet would be a small price to pay to see the look on Cerelia's face when Maia returned with a basket full of her favorite fruit.

As she followed the spider through the evergreens, Maia noticed new ferns shooting up through the melting snow and new light green needles on the trees. It had been two months since she had fled into the forest and ended up in the witch's garden. By her calculations, the world outside was nearing the end of summer and she hoped they wouldn't have to go too far outside of the enchanted forest to find what she was looking for.

She picked her way around a blackberry bush, keeping her eye out for the hoaxes that Cerelia had spoken of. On the other side of it, she spied a fae fox hiding behind a shrub. According to Cerelia, the foxes kept the hoaxes out of the garden.

She avoided the hoaxes, staying on the path where Xee led her. But the spider didn't avoid everything that was dangerous.

Maia caught the smell of something rotting as she climbed over a particularly large tree root. She slowed, wary about the source of the smell.

The body lay halfway beneath a fern, its legs twisted and the torso laid flat. Maia recognized the stretched, gray limbs of a rumple goblin.

"Xee…" She stepped back onto the path that she had just traveled with the spider and looked around. Had the rumples come for her? The tree branches swayed high above her where there was a constant breeze blowing in from the sea. Below that, the forest was rather quiet and bright in the morning light.

Xee climbed up the rumple goblin's legs and further up the torso that lay shadowed under the fern.

Maia stepped closer and peered at the body. Pockets had been carved out of the goblin's torso.

"Is it dead?" Maia nudged it with a leather-covered toe.

A greenish substance oozed from the pockets. A dead night fairy larva came out of one of the pockets with the express.

Maia felt sick. The goblin was definitely dead.

Mortal, mortal, here I be.

She understood now why the rumple goblins wanted to be immune to the night fairies' poison.

"I..." she didn't know exactly what to say. Xee climbed down from the rumple carcass and continued through the trees. With a deep breath, Maia settled the roiling in her stomach and forced herself to look away. "That's why they want my baby. That's about the most horrible way to die that I could imagine, and while I was chained down in the dungeon, I thought of some pretty horrible ways for Tom to die—boiled, burned, flayed, slow-roasted. Rumple Six fulfilled his part of the contract quickly. Tom's death was swift."

She glanced at the mark on her arm, the rest of what she had to say silenced by the satisfaction that came with the memory of Tom's eviscerated body in the little dungeon cell.

"You know, I've started to dream of her, Xee. Holding her in my arms, her tiny little face and her tiny little fingers. I've held babies before. I spent a few years living with Doni, the midwife. Earned my keep, too. There's good coin in keeping secrets. Our village was where the neighboring noblemen sent their daughters to whelp their bastards. And paid us to hide the evidence."

The spider shifted course slightly, still moving ahead at a good pace. Maia looked up. Something about the new direction felt familiar. Through the trees, she glimpsed the glint of the sun on water and realized she was headed in the direction of the village. She watched the shadows more carefully while reminding herself that she was still in the enchanted forest.

And certainly Xee would warn her if Lord Graves was anywhere near, wouldn't she?

The spider had stopped a short distance ahead, perched with her eight legs on top of a large, juicy strawberry. Maia grinned. The sun shone down right on the strawberry vines, the light bright where it came down through the final line of trees that edged a wide clearing.

Maia crouched, plucked a large, ripe strawberry, and took a bite. The juice dribbled down her chin as she filled the basket with more. "Oh, my stars! Look at these puckers! Quite a find, Xee. I knew you would do it. Cerelia will be thrilled! I can't wait to see her face when we get back with so many strawberries we can't eat them all. We'll slice them on our pancakes, make them into strawberry jam to have with our tea, and, let me tell you, I can bake the best strawberry tart this side of the royal dungeon. I learned baking from our own Miss Maudlin when she took me in for a year. I hate to brag, but I could bake a better tart than she ever could. She never had the proper patience to get that light, flaky dough."

Xee had morphed to the size of the red-breasted blackbirds that flittered in the trees above them. She snatched a strawberry with her pincers and nibbled the fruit to nothing while Maia watched. It might take her a hundred years to get used to the way the spider changed size like that.

More birds fluttered and chirped in the trees overhead. A robin hopped down from the lower branches of a fir and dug into a strawberry with its beak. In that moment, with the sun warming the snow and the birds dancing in the trees, Maia felt…happy.

The baby moved suddenly, a strong kick that made Maia's insides twinge.

"Oof!" Maia sat back on her heels and stretched her torso,

trying to give the baby a little more room. "That went straight into my spleen. She's strong, Xee."

She looked down at her rounding belly, smoothing a hand over the bulge beneath her skirt. Guilt twisted in her gut and bubbled up, wedging in her throat. Maia lifted her arm and pushed her sleeve to her elbow. The rumple mark that had been so faint when she'd first arrived at Cerelia's cottage that she could only make it out when it reflected the moonlight. Now it was a dark gold, easy to see even in the early morning shadows. She made a fist, flexing the muscle of her forearm. She could feel the mark, too, like a thread of silk tugging on her flesh.

"You know, Xee, I didn't want my daughter to be a secret. I wanted her to have a mother and a father and a home. I thought, with Tom, I could give her everything I never had. I forgot all that when Lord Graves turned the village against me." Tears trailed down her cheeks and dripped onto her arm. "Maybe the rumples won't be able to find me in Cerelia's garden."

She let the hope settle inside her for a moment before it broke apart and scattered inside her in useless pieces.

It was time to tell Cerelia about the rumples.

The spider had sidled away, heading toward the break in the trees. Maia reached for a few final strawberries to top off the already overflowing basket. Her hand came across something hard and smooth beneath the fat leaves of the strawberry vines. She pulled it out and held it up to get a better look. It was a small hatchet, the blade a little rusty but still relatively sharp, and the shaft was a bit weathered, but it would clean up with some light sanding.

"Hey, Xee—" Maia looked for the spider to show her what she had found. It took her a moment to spot the white body out in the sunshine. Beneath her, the ground looked...burnt.

Leaving her basket in the middle of the strawberry vines,

Maia wandered after the spider. As she stepped from the final shadows of the trees, her makeshift boots crunched on a carpet of charred leaves. The clearing cut its way through the trees like a great black scar.

Maia stepped carefully through the burnt debris, noticing all the new green shoots that were fighting their way through the layer. There was no snow here, nor was there any in the mix of fir and aspen trees on the other side. The winter that had been protecting the enchanted forest and Cerelia's garden ended here.

A few more steps and her foot caught on something heavier than burnt trees and vines. Looking down, Maia caught a glimpse of something that looked familiar. Not another rumple, but something that made her heart race.

She bent over and brushed away a layer of ash and charred wood from the insignia of the House of Graves.

She gasped and stepped back. She looked around, studying the shadows between the trees on the other side of the clearing. She recognized it all now. This was where Lord Graves and the villagers had chased her to the edge of the enchanted forest with their torches and their ropes.

What had happened here? Despite the determined growth of new green things, Maia was certain that whatever fire had burned the edge of the enchanted wood had happened shortly after she had run away and found Cerelia and her garden.

She crept closer to the insignia and brushed away more of the ash. It was indeed the symbol of the House of Lord Graves, woven into the leather of a vest. She brushed away even more ash to reveal a body that was half-burnt and half-decayed. Swallowing the bile that burned at the back of her throat, she uncovered more of one of Lord Graves's lackeys. He hadn't died from the fire, though. A giant thorn pierced his chest. Maia wrapped her fingers around it, closed her eyes, and pulled it out. The part that had been buried in flesh was still a gray-green, hard and sharp.

Cerelia.

Maia stood and backed away, dropping the thorn on the body. She gripped the hatchet tighter and looked for Xee. The spider had wandered off somewhere.

With a final glance at the body in the ash, Maia hurried back to her basket of strawberries. She snatched it up, the hatchet firmly in her other hand, and headed back through the enchanted forest toward the garden. Her footsteps showed up occasionally in the mud or in the snow and she could follow them.

A sense of unease lingered along her spine. The scene she had just left was clearly something that had happened between Lord Graves and Cerelia. Why hadn't Cerelia told her? When exactly had it happened?

Then a bubble of hope rose in her chest. What if Lord Graves himself had been killed?

Maia spotted the garden hedge up ahead through the trees, a thin spiral of smoke twisting out from the thatched roof of the cottage. The misgivings about the fire in the forest gave way to her excitement to surprise Cerelia with the strawberries.

As she approached, angry voices carried through the trees.

BLOOD FOR BLOOD

S eptaria slept on the cottage roof, her face tucked beneath her wing as the midmorning sun bathed the garden in light.

Cerelia climbed the vines with an ease that spoke of the last hundred years, although it had taken her more than a few of those years to understand the rhythms of the forest. She hadn't always had a gargoyle right there on her roof, and after the first one had built its nest there, it had cost her a few gashes and more than one tumble from the roof to learn how to get along with it.

The view from that height usually made her smile—the layered petal shapes of her garden labyrinth and the hedges defining the boundary and the forest beyond.

This morning what she saw sent a mix of dread and excitement through her. The snow was definitely melting. Several swaths of brown and green wove their way through the trees where it had been nothing but white except for their towering trunks and thick needles. She had been a prisoner for so long…

But, like the rabbit and the rampion, it meant the garden was vulnerable to mortals.

It had been years since she had dreamt of a world outside the garden. Now that Maia had come, she didn't know if she would want to leave. The girl was settling in. She even seemed happy. She was rounding out with the child, and she had good color in her cheeks and a layer of plumpness on her bones. Her hair had grown fast, golden and brown curls almost covering the back of her neck, and the scar on her cheek had faded to a deep pink.

The fact that Maia was out collecting strawberries as a surprise for Cerelia warmed her heart. It was hard to truly surprise Cerelia when Maia was using her familiar as a guide, and Cerelia would have sent the spider after her for protection anyway. She knew the strawberries grew along the burn scar, and even though Cerelia was fairly certain the nasty Lord Graves had died from the thorns that had pierced his armor, she had been denied the certainty and the satisfaction of having his corpse rotting along with those of his worthless henchmen.

She had fought off one threat. Cerelia wondered what it would take to get Maia to trust her enough to confide in her about the rumple mark on her arm. The mark had grown darker with each passing day, tracking time for the goblins. Cerelia had scoured her books for information on the rumples and their magic. Most of what she had found were fairy tales and legends with dregs of real information. What she had gleaned from those was that she needed to know exactly what was in Maia's contract with the manipulative little buggers. She had to find a loophole and she was running out of time.

The night fairy trap hung from a vine behind her, the night fairies just starting to wake from their drunken dragonberry stupor. Good. The gargoyle preferred a little bit of a chase over having the night fairies just plopped on the roof thatch.

She tapped Septaria's wing.

The creature raised her head enough to peer at Cerelia with one obsidian eye.

"I have some delicious treats for you, my stony friend. Would you like a night fairy feast this morning? I think I counted twelve. I ripened the entire bush and the little buggers simply can't resist." Cerelia tucked a finger in one of the vine bars of the trap and made it swing. One fairy looked up and stretched its wings, too groggy to know what was happening, and another climbed up to the trap door and tried to move the lever. The iron burned it and it grumbled in nonsense syllables.

The gargoyle lifted her wing from her face and yawned. She shifted to all fours and stretched her wings, then tucked them on her back and looked at Cerelia. Then she looked at the night fairies in the trap and licked her lips.

The night fairy that had tried to reach through the bars screeched and hopped to the far side of the trap.

"Wake your little friends," Cerelia told it. "I'll open the door and let you all out when you're ready to fly away."

The night fairy fluttered around, then perched on the pile of fairies that covered the floor of the trap and tugged at their ears and their wings.

The gargoyle stretched back like a dog, the stone texture of her flesh crackling in the morning light. Four eggs lay beneath her in her nest lined with the deep red and black petals of the reaper blossoms.

Cerelia gathered the eggs in her basket and smiled at the gargoyle. "Are you ready, Septaria?"

The gargoyle sat up, her wings half open, almost dancing in anticipation.

Cerelia lifted the bar from the trap door, and the night

fairies swarmed out in different directions. The gargoyle waited in a crouch, her eyes darting back and forth as she tracked their paths. In one smooth motion, she leapt from the cottage roof, her wings stretched wide, and she glided toward the trees. She snatched her first night fairy straight out of the air above the dragonberry bushes, swallowed it in a single gulp, and turned to follow the next one where it had landed in some fairy bells in a hungover stupor.

Sitting on the roof with her basket of eggs, Cerelia watched the gargoyle hunt until the creature disappeared somewhere over the hedge in the trees.

She wondered fleetingly if Maia's baby would grow up to like gargoyle eggs, then shook the thought from her mind. She would be careful not to be too hopeful about that. There was too much uncertainty hanging over the situation for her to give in to the joy of it.

She heard some clanking below, the steady thud of metal on earth, and caught flashes of people marching toward the cottage garden.

Not just people. The people from Maia's village. And in front of them all, wearing the same armor he had when Cerelia had fought him a couple months before, was Lord Graves. He moved stiffly. The thorns that had pierced him should have killed him, but there he was, an evil that refused to die.

Cerelia watched as they approached, looking further into the trees for Maia. She sent a warning to Xee, hoping the spider would keep the girl away until this was over, no matter how it ended.

Lord Graves and his followers stopped at the stone wall. There were seven of them total, five men and two women, carrying pitchforks, rope, and a couple buckets of water.

"Witch in the Woods! Where is the girl? Give her up and I will reward you with a swift death," Lord Graves demanded, pointing his scepter toward Cerelia. He flinched as he moved.

At least he was still in pain.

She settled the basket of eggs on a little hook formed by the vine and waved it away. The vine moved as Cerelia willed it, carrying the precious goods down to the stoop of the cottage door. Another vine carried her to the ground. She wove her way through her garden until she stood far enough in on the garden side of the hedge that Lord Graves could not quite reach her with his sword.

"Ah, and who has come calling in my woods? Perhaps we shall save our demands until after we have had a proper introduction." Cerelia studied the faces of the villagers carefully as the pompous lord approached, watching them for flashes of fear. Her stomach twisted. All she saw were looks of cruel determination. These would be the bravest of the villagers who would have ventured this far into the enchanted woods, the zealous ones who had fully discarded any care they had for Maia as one of their own. The ones who wouldn't stop until the girl was dead and they had appeased the insanity of this tyrant.

She hoped the villagers had stopped outside the hedge because they could sense the magic that protected the garden, even if it was shifting. Still, she didn't know if it would be enough to keep them from crossing the boundary. "I am Cerelia, the Witch in the Woods as you called me. Lord Graves, I presume? You are exactly as Maia described you. Small, insecure, and nurturing an overdeveloped sense of loathing."

Lord Graves clanked the scepter against the thigh plate of his armor, sneering at her with disgust. "I am Lord Alabaster Graves! The fifth unsullied generation of direct descendants from the First King himself! I have come for the girl you have been harboring in this...this *hovel* you call a home. She owes me a blood debt on which I fully intend to collect."

As if on cue, the villagers behind him each took a small step forward, their hands tightening on the pitchfork shafts and their coils of rope.

"We're practically neighbors, Lord Graves. I have lived here peacefully for over a hundred years and you've never come calling. I must say that is quite a disappointing lack of decorum in a descendant of the First King. Might I invite you in for tea? Get to know my unwarranted adversary before you cut out my heart? Or whatever it is you plan to do?" Cerelia sent her tendrils of magic into the ground, connecting to the plants in the garden that she raised like her own children. They responded, vines from the cottage walls quietly trailing through the reaper blossoms that were slowly expanding in size. The dragonberries shifted and the fox shrubs wove their branches together.

Deep within the center of the garden, Cerelia could feel the rapid beating of her heart.

The villagers glanced around, sensing that something was happening.

Lord Graves, however, kept his gaze squarely on Cerelia. He drew his sword and stepped up to the arched opening in the hedge, one foot just crossing the line that Cerelia could not.

Cerelia enjoyed the small sense of satisfaction she felt at seeing the holes in his armor where her thorns had pierced it.

He pointed his blade at her. "I plan to run this entire length of steel through you, and then I'll do the same to the girl. Do you know what she did to my Tom?"

Xee climbed up Cerelia's skirt to her shoulder.

A flutter of motion caught Cerelia's attention, back in the trees behind Lord Graves and his crew.

Maia.

Cerelia hoped the girl had enough sense to stay put until this was over, no matter how it ended. She held Lord Graves's rage-filled eyes. The only blessing about the fact that he was still alive was that she now had a chance to tell him a few things. "I know she ran for her life, and the life of her unborn child, after *your* Tom abandoned her to your fear and your ego like the selfish ogre you raised him to be. I know she had her heart rent to pieces when your threats ran through the villagers like a pestilence and they turned against her, too. I know that you took a young, confused girl who once believed in love despite the fact that she had no true home and tried to turn her into a martyr for your rotten soul. Yes, Lord Graves. I know what she did to *your* Tom. I know that he deserved it, too. As do you."

Lord Graves's face had turned so red while Cerelia spoke that he looked like an overripe dragonberry that would pop at the slightest scratch from a night fairy.

"Tom was nothing but a mass of flesh when we found him in the dungeon. There's no way a girl of her size, unarmed, could have done that to another human. We know she had the help of demons, called by her magic. She has to die, and so do you." He shifted his weight forward on the foot that was on the garden boundary line and the silent buzzing increased.

Cerelia tensed, willing her plants to wait. She could feel them feeding on her emotions, ready to twist and pierce and bite. But she had a thin hope that this battle still might be won with words. "She didn't call any demons. She signed a contract with a rumple goblin. That's what happened to your Tom. She was so desperate that she was willing to sign away her unborn child. If you think you are upset over the insult of your son's well-deserved fate, imagine how much rage Maia is harboring toward you if she is willing to give up her child to escape your clutches. Balance is the first law of magic, Lord Graves. You cannot take something without giving something in return. You took Maia's freedom, dignity, and more. Tom was the price, and a bargain at that. You can leave now and things will remain even, but if you insist on creating another debt, this time it will be you who will pay the price. Along with the six fools standing behind you."

Lord Graves's blade fell a little. He turned his head and looked at the villagers behind him. Cerelia hoped he saw the same uncertainty that she did on their dirty faces.

After a moment, he turned his eyes back to her.

Cerelia held the plants ready.

Then Lord Graves lunged through the open archway and into the garden, sinking his sword into Cerelia's chest.

11

HUSH NOW, DARLING

Cerelia cried out, the sound something between a scream and a sigh. The vines curled around Cerelia in support, covering the wound and applying pressure. Blood ran down Cerelia's dress and over some of the wide vine leaves. She felt the plants' fear, and their anger.

She heard Maia scream.

Lord Graves swung his blade at anything green, held back by vines that were twisted around his legs and waist, yelling orders. "Find her! Find the girl but save her for me! I want to see the life drain from her eyes after I run my sword through her."

Three of the villagers swarmed into the garden. They brandished their pitchforks and their buckets, grabbing their ears as the magical buzzing increased to a painful pitch. One woman tripped over a twist of vine, her bucket of holy water tumbling toward the reaper blossoms and leaving a path of hissing poison in its wake. A reaper blossom loomed up, having expanded to the size of a human adult, and snatched her up whole.

Another villager was caught in the dragonberry bushes

like in a standing coffin, the branches squeezing the air out of him after he'd sunk his pitchfork into the cottage wall.

The third villager who had crossed the barrier was out of sight when Cerelia heard a squelch and received a sense of satisfaction from Xee.

The vines pulled Cerelia back to the heart of the garden. She fought the pain in her shoulder, forcing herself to focus. Her beloved garden was fighting back, directed by her magic but driven by its own will to survive and to protect her. She grew thorns out on a length of the vine and sent it like a whip through two of the villagers who still stood outside the hedge. They had turned to hunt down Maia as their lord demanded. The whip caught one in the throat. The other ducked and the vine missed him.

The final villager ran but didn't get very far. The gargoyle swooped out of the trees and dug her claws into his shoulders. They crashed into the lower branches of a fir tree, the man screaming in pain.

Lord Graves fought his way through the vines, his expression seething with righteous vengeance. "I'll have you! I will have the girl! I will destroy you both!"

Cerelia smiled. She could feel the blood on her teeth and taste it on her tongue. "You already sent Maia to Hell, Lord Graves. And Hell did not want her. Hell sent her back with a message for you."

Lord Graves paused, his sword half-raised, a look of uncertainty on his face. Cerelia even caught the flash of fear in his eyes as he looked around.

The villagers who had followed their lord into this misguided campaign had all fallen.

He was alone.

"Where is she?" He raised the sword to Cerelia's throat the flat of it lifting her chin. "You're already dead. My blade went straight through your damned heart. Looks like I get to kill you twice."

He should have sounded more confident for the position he claimed he was in, but a tremor in Lord Graves's voice betrayed his fear.

Cerelia caught movement behind him, the sun shining on Maia's curls. Cerelia kept her eyes focused on the man holding his sword to her neck, careful not to betray the girl coming up behind him.

"Where is the little witch?" Lord Graves asked, his voice louder with a forced confidence. "I will send her and her demon spawn to a place where they will be less than nothing. She should have stayed in Hell whether Hell wanted her or not."

There was a squelching, crunching sound and Lord Graves spun around. The sword fell as he turned, missing Cerelia's throat and cutting down through her collarbone.

A hatchet stuck out from his back, the blade wedged in the gap of his armor between his spine and his shoulder blade.

His arm jutted out and his gauntleted hand clamped around Maia's throat. He lifted the girl off the ground, her face quickly turning red then purple. She clawed at the metal covering his hand.

"Ah, so nice of you to arrive on to time to your death. I imagined running my blade through your heart as I did to your accomplice behind me. But I find the gradually increasing fear in your eyes to be far more satisfying. You do not deserve a quick death after what you did to Tom." His arm started to shake with Maia's weight.

As he spoke, Cerelia sent a vine up behind him, the length of it climbing up the backplate of his armor and then twisting around his throat. It cinched tight and he dropped

Maia, tearing ineffectively at the woody tendril with metal fingers.

Maia only took a second to catch her breath. The expression on her face darkened to an utter, consuming rage. Lord Graves dropped to his knees. Maia moved behind him, and shoving a leather-clad foot against his back for leverage, pulled the hatchet out.

She looked at Cerelia and nodded.

Cerelia released the vine.

Before Lord Graves gained his feet, Maia swung the hatchet straight into his throat. "Hell has been waiting for you. Say hello to Tom for me."

Blood flowed down his breast plate. His eyes shifted from shock to anger, narrowing as they focused on Maia. He opened his mouth to speak, but his lips didn't seem to be working. The only sound he made was a strange gurgling noise.

Then he fell to the ground, his legs bent behind him at an awkward angle.

Dead.

Cerelia slumped into the vines that held her. They were the only thing keeping her upright. She struggled to keep her eyes open, even with the sensations and sounds of Xee's pincers crunching through flesh and bone and the anger that still flowed through her garden.

"Maia," Cerelia reached out a hand.

The girl stepped close, placing Cerelia's palm against her cheek. Tears ran down her face, streaking a path through the blood spray. "I'm sorry I wasn't fast enough to keep him from hurting you." Her eyes wandered down to the blood-soaked leaves covering Cerelia's wound and gasped. "Your heart!"

Cerelia managed a weak smile. "The garden is my heart. It will heal me. And Lord Graves will never return, Maia. You did that, brave girl. You saved us both."

Maia's tears ran harder. "Cerelia…"

Cerelia let her eyes close. The vines carried her to the center of the garden and laid her down inside the ring of gnomeshrooms and stones. She listened to the beat of her heart in the earth beneath her, like a lullaby, as her plants wrapped around her like a cocoon.

Maia clawed and pulled at the vines enclosing Cerelia's body. She could hardly breathe. It was as if the vines were wrapping around her, too, crushing her lungs.

They couldn't take Cerelia. Maia *needed* her.

Desperation bloomed in Maia's chest. She picked up the hatchet, ready to chop through the vine cocoon, when a vine twisted up and pulled the small weapon from her grip.

She watched with wide eyes as the vines moved like a hundred serpents over Lord Graves's body, twisting in through the gaps in his armor and rending the metal to scrap.

Not just the armor, but Lord Graves, too. As the metal tore away, Maia heard Lord Graves's limbs being ripped from his body, strange and wet like the sound she had heard when Six had turned Tom into nothing but a pile of innards. Blood soaked into the honey clover and the fairy bells and ran in pools beneath the reaper blossoms before it stained the ground beneath them. Bones crunched inside the pieces of armor, crushed by the vines as they carried the scraps of Lord Graves out of the garden.

It was happening in the rest of the garden, too. The vines were destroying and removing all of the villagers who had come to kill them.

So much red…

Maia fell to her knees beside Cerelia's cocoon. Grief

threatened to tear her apart just as the vines tore Lord Graves apart. It wound through her arms and legs and ribs until every inch of her was screaming. She flung herself over the mound, holding it as closely as she could, willing the vines to release the woman who had become her mother.

She cried, great wracking sobs that shook her whole body. The baby responded, kicking and stretching restlessly. It was the only thing that pulled Maia out of the deep void of grief that threatened to swallow her.

By the time Maia looked up from the mound, night had settled over the garden. She traced her fingertips over the vines and whispered through a wave of fresh tears, "Come back to me, Cerelia. Please. I need you. You are the truest mother I have ever known. Please."

And then, around her, it was as if the stars were suddenly on the ground. They blinked for a heartbeat, then rose up in the twinkling of pearlescent drops.

Maia sucked in a breath of joy. She plucked one of the Tears of Midnight from the air.

Oh, child. Not all tears are from sadness and pain. We can also shed tears of joy, Maia. Even when it feels like our darkest hour.

12

BY THE LAW OF THREE

L ord Graves's gauntlet and scepter sat on Maia's lap, the shiny steel splattered with dirt and blood. His sword had been taken by the vines along with his armor, but they had left her these.

Her trophies.

She thought that she would feel bad for killing someone with her own hands, that guilt and horror would come flooding in after her grief for Cerelia had made a sliver of space for any other emotion, but all it gave her was a deep sense of satisfaction. She'd spent time staring at the gauntlet every day for the last three days while she waited for Cerelia to emerge from her living cocoon.

He had deserved to die. He had deserved to have that hatchet buried deep in his throat where he could no longer spew the venom that had cost her Tom and the people she loved. The venom that had cost her everything she'd ever known. He had deserved to have his body torn to pieces by the same vines that loved Cerelia.

But still, Lord Graves's voice haunted her waking hours in the quiet peace of the garden.

Witch.

While she stared at the gauntlet, she remembered the look in his eyes as he realized that he had lost. All his lies and witch hunting and in the end he had been the one on his knees with his blood pouring out of him.

Xee climbed onto Maia's knee. The spider had spent a day sleeping beneath the dragonberry bushes and then had gone about her business in the garden as if everything were completely normal.

"How much longer?" Maia asked her.

Xee lifted her front legs in answer.

Maia sighed. "Okay, I'll wait."

Moving the spider to her shoulder, she set the gauntlet down next to the hatchet and fetched her sewing from the bed. She had gone through Cerelia's trunk and the fabric scraps folded neatly on a shelf, and she had started to sew baby clothes. She knew, somehow, that the baby was a girl. She'd known almost from the beginning, understanding what the midwife had always said about a mother's intuition.

Keeping busy was the only way she hadn't gone crazy while Cerelia was cocooned. She had made the strawberries into everything she knew how: strawberry jam, strawberry jelly, little strawberry tarts with perfect flaky crusts, strawberry bread, dried strawberries, and even strawberry syrup.

Then she had turned to sewing baby clothes while she watched the sun go by overhead and ate the rampion that had started to sprout all through the garden. She craved it so badly that she ate almost nothing else.

Xee climbed down onto Maia's arm.

Maia slid thread through some linen that she had cut from an old shift she had found in the trunk. She had learned to sew from the village seamstress, Doni, who had thankfully not been in the witch-hunting group with Lord Graves.

Still, Maia had known all the villagers who had come for her head. She would not mourn them.

The spider moved onto the linen in Maia's lap as if asking what it was for.

Maia smiled, although deep down she knew she was pretending that she would ever get to hold her child when the rumples came. "It is for the baby, Xee. The little ones like to be wrapped tightly. We'll have to make some blankets next. And swaddling. And—"

There was a sound outside, as if something were scratching at the door. Xee scurried off Maia's lap.

The door swung open, and Cerelia burst inside. The front of her dress was covered in dried blood, her eyes bright. "Maia! Oh, my rosebuds, I'm famished. Do we have any gargoyle eggs? I could eat a dozen. And dragonberry wine?"

"You're alive!" Maia hadn't realized that despite all the signs, she had been truly scared that Cerelia might actually be dead.

"Oh, Maia! I feel great. Like I'm a full decade younger. I should take a nap like that more often." She shoved half a strawberry tart in her mouth, crumbs from the crust falling over the blood stain on her dress. "It's like I died and went to strawberry heaven."

"You were asleep for *three days*." Maia stared at Cerelia. She couldn't decide if she should cry or shout for joy or both. She rocked forward in the chair but still struggled to get up. She scooted to the edge and tried again. This time, she made it to her feet. "It looks like Lord Graves stabbed you directly in the heart."

Cerelia nodded. "He stabbed me where my heart used to be. I told you, it's in the center of the garden."

Maia remembered the first full moon she helped Cerelia in the garden, when the witch had surprised her with the Tears of Midnight. Cerelia had stepped to the hedge, beneath one of the archways, and stretched her hand out into the moonlight. Then she had snatched it back as if it had caused her pain. "That's why you can't leave, isn't it? Your heart is here."

Opening a jar of strawberry jam and digging into it with a spoon, Cerelia nodded. "Yes. In return, the garden has protected me. But something has changed."

"Because of me. You said the magic has shifted." Maia sat on the bed. Standing for too long was starting to hurt her back.

"Yes, and I think I know why." Cerelia licked jelly from her lips and set the jar down. She sat next to Maia. She lifted Maia's wrist and pulled back her sleeve.

Maia cringed at the sight of the rumple mark. It had a gold sheen to it when it caught the light, reminiscent of the fire that had burned through Maia when she had eaten Six's strawberry rhubarb tart. It had grown darker every day, the shift so subtle that Maia hadn't realized that until she had gone to gather the strawberries.

Instinctively, she pulled away. "You knew. I was going to tell you when I came back with the strawberries."

"It's hard to hide magic from a witch, Maia. I was waiting for you to trust me enough to tell me, but we don't have time." Cerelia picked up Maia's arm again and traced the mark with her fingers, sending a buzzing through Maia's arm. It was as if Cerelia's touch agitated the magic. "With the rumple mark, I think the magic was confused. Nothing mortal was allowed to enter the garden. I rarely even saw a mortal creature near the garden even beyond the hedge. You are a mortal carrying magic, even though the magic is not yours. I do believe that shifted some part of the balance that this garden has maintained for, what did you say from the marks on the door? Over a hundred years?"

She let Maia's arm go, the mark still tingling.

Maia tugged her sleeve back down. "The way you fought Lord Graves and the villagers...we can do that with the rumples, too? I saw the other side of the forest when I was out collecting strawberries. I could tell you fought them there. I found one of ..." She hesitated. Killing Lord Graves had felt right. His death had given Maia a sense of redemption, of righting a wrong. But stumbling over the burned forest gave Maia a feeling of sadness. She rubbed her hand along her belly. One small life had cost so many.

"I know," Cerelia finished for her. "That was right after you came here. I did what I could from so far away. Lord Graves was injured when they dragged him away and I thought...hoped...that he was dead when the villagers didn't return."

Maia grabbed Cerelia's hand. "But you still did it. You fought them off again and they won't be back. Even after Lord Graves stabbed you. You're powerful, Cerelia. Powerful enough to fight off the rumples when they come. I know you are. I heard what you said to Lord Graves about balance being the first law of magic. I know you can find a way to bargain with the rumples."

Cerelia pulled her hand from Maia's and stood from the bed.

Maia's heart sank. This is not what she had wanted Cerelia's reaction to be about the rumples. She had wanted Cerelia to smile at her and tell her that everything was going to be okay. That they could defeat the rumples and save her baby.

She wanted Cerelia to brush her hair behind her ear like a mother and tell her that they were going to live in the garden forever as a happy family.

Instead, Cerelia frowned as she walked over to her books, half of them covered by some form of strawberry concoction. She fished one out from under a handful of jars and brought it back to the bed.

The book was heavy across Maia's lap as Cerelia opened it and fished through the pages until she found one that had a drawing of the same mark that was on Maia's arm. "It took me awhile to find this. I knew I had seen it somewhere before. It is very clear how binding a rumple contract is. Their magic is very old and strong."

"But so is yours," Maia pleaded with Cerelia. "You are more powerful than you believe. Your love has saved us all, even you."

"Yes, I have magic, Maia. It is a gift from this forest, and it came at a great cost." Cerelia frowned. The vibrance she'd had when she had burst into the cottage had dimmed.

"Your heart." Maia's own heart skipped a beat.

"Yes, my heart, but there's more than that," Cerelia fought tears and swallowed before she continued. "I had a baby girl."

As Cerelia spoke, Maia heard a soul-deep pain in her voice.

"She was so beautiful, so tiny and perfect and mine." Cerelia looked away, at the orbs that hung from the vines that twisted beneath the thatch of the roof, or at the fireplace or the stack of books and strawberry-filled jars. But Maia could tell her mind went somewhere else, reliving her memories. "I loved a woodcutter's son, so long ago I don't even remember his name. It's almost as if that part of the story doesn't matter anymore."

Maia's hand wandered to her belly where the baby kicked, and she thought of Tom. Would she have a chance to tell their daughter his name? Maybe it was something that would be best for Maia to forget. Let his name die along with him and his evil. Her child would never know that there was ever a time when she had not been loved and wanted.

Cerelia's fingers absentmindedly fidgeted with the pages

of the book on their laps. "I thought my father loved me enough that he would understand when he came home from campaigning for the king. He arrived while I was giving birth. I heard him tell one of his soldiers to feed my baby to the wolves and send me to a convent. He said he never wanted to see me again. So, as soon as the midwife had swaddled her and handed her to me and left the room, I held her tight and ran. It was early winter and we were still waiting for snow. I was in my birthing gown, barefoot. But there was so much blood we couldn't hide from the hounds."

She fell silent, her eyes brimming with tears. She swallowed hard, as if fighting to keep her emotions in check.

Tears threatened in Maia's own eyes. Memories of the night that the rumples killed Tom flashed through her mind. The flames of the torches. Their chant of *Witch! Witch!* and the despising looks on their faces, as if she were some contagious evil.

The fear from that night tightened around her lungs.

Clearing her throat, Cerelia continued. "I don't know how I made it this far, Maia. I should have been caught outside the manor, but the hounds had been my friends and they didn't know what to do when they found me. This garden is where my legs gave out and I knew I couldn't run anymore. I begged the forest to protect us in exchange for my heart. And the forest agreed. It took my heart and my daughter, but at least here we were together. In this little space where it is always summer and mortal beings could not enter."

"Until now." Guilt replaced the fear from Maia's memories, a heavier feeling, lower in her gut.

Cerelia nodded. "Something shifted the moment that you signed the contract. That night, before you ran into my garden, I saw a stag out in the trees. I hadn't seen one in over a century. It was as if the forest gave me a sign that you were coming."

Maia traced the rumple mark on the page. The space around it was filled with writing in a language that Maia didn't recognize, but it had the same scrolling flourish as the magical golden writing that had been on the rumple contract.

"We can fight the rumples, though, right? We can try?" The desperation in Maia's heart was reflected in her voice.

Finally, Cerelia met her eyes. "We will try, Maia. But I want to be honest with you. This book is very clear that there is no way *out* of a rumple contract. They will be coming for your baby."

Tears fell down Maia's cheeks. Quiet tears that dripped from her chin to her growing belly. She looked down where her baby was becoming stronger every day.

Blood for blood.

13

RUMPLE, RUMPLE

"Call him," Cerelia said. It was halfway between an encouraging request and a command. She could see the fear on Maia's face, the uncertainty.

It had to be done.

"Call him," Cerelia repeated.

They stood in the middle of the garden over Cerelia's heart. The rampion was growing wild there now, tall and vivid green even in the mist of twilight. Maia had been eating it as if her life depended on it.

Xee crawled around between the stalks, her white body reflecting the last dregs of sunlight that lingered over the forest.

Maia nodded. "Rumple, rumple, hear my plight," she began.

"Louder," Cerelia ordered. She could feel her heartbeat beneath her feet. She was anxious, calling on some of the most ancient magic of which she had ever learned. The rumple goblins were one of this world's first magical creatures and their magic used an energy that Cerelia couldn't even touch.

She had cleared the night fairies from the garden in preparation for calling the rumples. The gargoyle had helped hunt the few that lingered in the trees after the night's full moon.

Other than what plant magic Cerelia could muster at a moment's notice, they were completely defenseless, and she didn't think that plant magic would be particularly effective against a goblin.

"Rumple, rumple, hear my plight," Maia spoke louder this time, one hand hovering protectively around her belly and the other by her side. She only had one moon left before the baby would come, if that.

Cerelia watched the trees, sensed the energy in the garden. Nothing.

"Call him like you did that night, as if your life depended on it." Cerelia tried to keep her voice more encouraging. Maia was on edge. Cerelia sensed that her fear of the rumples was very different than her fear of Lord Graves had been.

Maia took a deep breath. "Rumple! Rumple! Hear my plight! Come to me this curs-ed night!"

The girl stood silent, biting her lip. She gave Cerelia a worried look.

"Finish it!" Cerelia ordered.

Maia looked out into the trees. "Rumple! Rumple! Hear my plight! Come to me this curs-ed night! A bargain now I'll make with thee! Take my babe and set me free!"

At first, the only response was a drifting echo that bounced off the trees. Cerelia held her breath, sensing that something in the air was shifting.

There was a shimmer before them, as if the air were suddenly water, and then a rumple goblin took shape. He looked like the illustrations in Cerelia's books, not too tall but somehow as if everything on his body had been stretched. He wore a red wool cap, and his eyes were almost completely black.

"Mortal, mortal, here I be, come to hear your desperate plea." His voice was high pitched and scratchy, as if even his vocal cords had been unnaturally stretched like the rest of him. "Blood for blood will end your plight; signed by soul this curs-ed night!"

"Six." Maia took a step back.

"You called?" The rumple goblin clasped his hands in front of him. "Do you need us to take care of a problem? Blood for blood will require another payment, and I'm not sure your mortal frame will survive the conclusion of our first contract."

The goblin didn't even look at Cerelia.

"It's about the first contract," Maia began, stealing a glance at Cerelia.

The rumple raised the skin above his eye where a human eyebrow would have been. As far as Cerelia could tell, there was no hair on the goblin's body.

"I want to make a deal," Maia stated. Her voice was steady but her lip quivered.

"And what do you propose? Is there another child you may leverage?" He gestured toward Cerelia. "Certainly not from her. She is barren."

The observation stung a little, but Cerelia had not convinced Maia to call the goblins here to offer them a child. She had wanted them here to decipher the contract. She needed to know what it said if they were going to have a chance of finding some way to manipulate the terms.

Maia took another deep breath. Her body quivered, tense, as if she were fighting the urge to run. "The contract said, 'Blood for blood,' correct?"

Six nodded once. "That is correct, mortal."

"It did not specify an infant child?" Maia pushed.

The goblin glowered.

Cerelia felt a charge in the air, as if the goblin were tapping into the source of his magic. She looked around behind Six, beyond the hedge, and made out at least two other shimmering shapes in the air.

Three goblins. They had come prepared for a fight.

Six finally answered Maia's question. "The contract was for an infant child, given over willingly by the mother."

"Body and soul?" Cerelia asked, hoping to pin the goblin down to more concrete details.

Grinning tightly, Six looked at Cerelia with wide black eyes. "I have nothing to discuss with you, witch. My contract is with the mortal girl."

"Body and soul?" Maia repeated Cerelia's question.

"We have no need for a human soul, but we do need the flesh to be fresh and tender. It is difficult to keep such delicate flesh alive without the soul inside. It is this gift of the mother that holds the magic, but only for a brief window of time after the child is born. I will return to collect the baby in one month." Six looked at Cerelia now. "You have our gratitude for clearing the night fairies from your garden before our arrival."

Cerelia nodded. "You're welcome. We would also welcome a return of any such favors of protection."

A sly grin crept onto Six's face. "We do not do favors. We fulfill contracts. We left her precious Tom Graves at her feet as a gift."

"Balance," Cerelia puzzled through the goblin's words and what she knew of magic. The rumple chant ran through her mind. 'Blood for blood' was for the babe, and it was very clear that Six had no intention to consider an alternative. But the child's soul was only important until the goblin had its flesh.

It was not the child's soul that was bound to the contract, it was Maia's.

The gargoyle fluttered her wings on the roof, watching Six and the two rumple shimmers with keen black eyes. Cerelia hoped Septaria would stay put. The last thing they needed was for fight to break out that ended the negotiation.

As hopeless as it seemed, at least Six was listening. And the gargoyle gave Cerelia an idea.

"Would it fulfill your contract if we found another mother who would willingly gift her child in place of Maia's?" Cerelia watched as the rumple goblin seemed to consider the possibility.

After a moment, he sneered. "My dear witch, you are not as clever as you think you are. The magic binds us as much by the intention of the contract as the words. This is the only child, the only human flesh that will satisfy this contract."

Six reached out toward Maia, a hungry look on his face.

Maia took a step back. "Don't touch me. She's still mine. You can't have her yet."

Cerelia moved to intervene, but the goblin set his hand on Maia's belly before she could close the distance.

Maia stumbled back, then dropped to her knees next to a reaper plant to catch her unbalanced weight. As Six settled his hands on her belly, his face twisted with greed, she reached beneath the broad leaves and swung the hatchet up from behind her and brought it down on his arm.

Six screamed and stumbled back, clutching the gash where Maia had nearly severed his arm beneath the elbow.

The two other goblins materialized just outside the hedge. They were at least three times as large as Six. They hissed, showing off a row of long pointed teeth.

And then they charged.

Cerelia ran to Maia. She grabbed the hatchet and pulled Maia to her feet. "Run! Into the cottage!"

Maia looked at her blankly, the blood from the goblin's arm splattered over her face.

"Run!" Cerelia screamed at her.

As if waking slowly from a nightmare, Maia turned her head toward the larger rumples, one of which held Six in its arms and the other who was charging at them.

No, it was charging at Cerelia.

"No!" Maia stepped between them.

Cerelia saw her grit her teeth as the large goblin halted a few feet away. Then Maia gasped. Cerelia saw the mark on Maia's forearm start to glow.

Gathering the energy of the garden, Cerelia brought a row of vines from the earth on either side of the rumple. They twisted up and wrapped around his ankles and wrists.

"Stop the vines, Cerelia. Don't fight. He can't hurt me," Maia explained to Cerelia while her eyes never wavered from the rumple. "That's one thing I figured out. The contract is with Six. No other rumples can jeopardize it."

With a sick feeling of fear, Cerelia did as Maia said and released the vines.

The goblin stood still but lowered his face until it was within a few inches of Maia's. With a sniff and a grunt, it turned and walked away.

Cerelia and Maia watched as the three rumples shimmered into nothing.

"Are you okay?" Cerelia wrapped her arms around Maia as the girl slumped to the ground. "Did he hurt you?"

As Cerelia wiped the blood from Maia's cheeks, tears began to stream down the girl's cheeks. The girl who had been so confident and fearless during the confrontation with the goblins felt so frail in Cerelia's arms.

"I don't want them to take my baby. Please, Cerelia. They can't. We have to stop them." She sobbed into Cerelia's shoulder, clutching at her so hard that it almost hurt.

Cerelia held her there, both of them sitting on the honey clover with goblin blood smeared over them and the hatchet lying beneath a demon fruit tree, until Maia's sobs faded to sniffles and she fell asleep in Cerelia's arms.

It was night.

The moon would be full in two days, and by the following full moon, Maia's baby would be born. Cerelia crept from the cottage while Maia slept. The girl had cried most of that day, sleeping in restless bouts and waking from nightmares only to do it all over again.

When Maia was sleeping, Cerelia had studied more about the rumples. She hoped she had missed something, some small detail in their magic that would help her find a way to keep the child, even if it meant sacrificing herself.

There was nothing. Not a single small hope in the ancient texts.

She would give anything to see Maia happy, her baby in her arms. She would give anything for Maia to have what Cerelia never did—the chance to raise her daughter, to watch her grow into a strong woman and fall in love and become a mother herself.

Settling amidst the rampion that had nearly taken over the fairy ring in the center of the garden, Cerelia looked around at what had been her entire world for over a century.

There, where she could feel the beat of her heart beneath the earth, the memories always followed. This time, they were all of Maia. The first night the girl had stumbled through the hedge that surrounded the garden, her face cut open and blood everywhere, Cerelia had known that the life she'd known was never going to be the same. In the weeks during which Maia had healed, she had brought a light to

Cerelia's life that had been dimmed ever since Cerelia's baby had been taken by the forest.

She had to find a way to save Maia's baby.

Looking at the moon, Cerelia stood and walked beneath the demon fruit trees and through the fairy bells to the hedge. With a deep breath, she stepped beneath an archway and stretched out her arm.

After several breaths, nothing happened.

Two more steps and she stood outside the garden. The ground was cold but not freezing. Most of the snow was gone, now, and the forest was taking on the greens of warmer weather.

She curled her toes on the bare earth and took a deep breath of the crisp night air.

Then suddenly she couldn't breathe. The air in her lungs felt like fire and her skin felt like it was melting. She bent over from the pain, falling to her knees. The flesh on her hands was as transparent as the moonlight, the bones of her fingers curled like the claws of a gargoyle.

With every ounce of strength she could muster through the pain, Cerelia crawled back into the garden. It seemed like all the hundred years of her existence passed again by the time she made it back into her garden.

After a moment, the fire in her lungs subsided enough that she could take a breath. She lay on her side, her cheek pressed to the honey clover, her face halfway beneath the fairy bells.

She was back in her garden.

As long as she was confined within its boundaries, she would not be able to follow when the rumples came for Maia's baby. She would have to find a way to outsmart them, find a way to save the child's soul even if she could not save its flesh.

14

THE ESSENCE OF THE OTHER

Maia held up the little doll she was making out of rampion from the center of the garden. It was almost finished.

This was the decoy that she and Cerelia had planned for the rumples to take when they came.

She added a few more stalks, checking the shape of the doll. She slipped a strip of fabric inside the doll's hollow torso. She had carefully stitched the rumple mark onto the linen with golden thread that Cerelia had blessed with a spell. When the fabric was securely nestled inside the little rampion body, Maia looked at the rumple mark on her own arm. The memory of the way it had burned when she had called Six still echoed in her flesh.

The rumple mark was not quite the final element to completing the spell. They still had one more thing they had to do in order for it to hold enough of her baby's essence to have a chance at fooling the goblins.

Maia wished there was another way. She would gladly give her own life for the one inside of her to have a future beyond being a rumple meal. She had spent a lot of her dreams on the regret and the possibilities. She had wished that she could turn back time and reverse her decision and never call the rumples in the first place.

She had also dreamed of a beautiful little girl with her golden curls weaving a crown of flowers in Cerelia's hair. That day, she woke with a face wet with tears. If only…

In her most desperate attempt to right her wrong, she had even pierced her arm with one of Cerelia's knives to see how deep the rumple mark went, hoping she could cut it out. All that did was send a shot of pain like lightning from her arm to her womb and made the baby frantic. Maia still hadn't forgiven herself.

Cerelia had studied her books exhaustively, searching for some way to manipulate the contract. She had woken Maia more than once, repeating 'blood for blood' while she studied the texts by the light of a vine orb.

The hatchet leaned against the wall beside the door. Maia had wanted it close in case the rumples came early and without warning. She had cleaned the blood off and sharpened it every day. She closed her eyes against the memory of swinging the blade down onto Six's arm. She had watched the look on his face shift to that of a perverted, insatiable hunger, his eyes wide and his teeth flashing. She had reacted when he'd reached for her. The blood that splattered on her face had stung a little and left behind tiny burn marks over the ragged pink scar on her cheek.

Lord Graves's gauntlet sat in a niche in the vines. She wished she had put the hatchet into Six's skull the same way she had put it into Lord Graves's. Then all her enemies would be dead.

The baby kicked hard. Maia grunted from the impact to her bladder.

"Oh, my precious daughter. Lord Graves, Six…Tom…" Tears choked her as she spoke the last name. "So much blood shed over something that was supposed to be a symbol of love. Why do you frighten them all so much when you should bring the world nothing but joy?"

Her only answer was the buzz of hive fairy wings.

Outside, it was a beautiful day. The snow in the forest beyond the garden had completely melted, and the forest itself was showing signs of late summer. Something about that made Cerelia restless, a deeper sense of unease and anticipation than the coming rumples. Maia could see her agitation in the shifting of her eyes and the constant motion in her hands.

The garden had been rearranged and rearranged again as Cerelia planned how to set it up for defense against the rumples. The herbs had been replaced with burrs that twisted themselves deeper into the skin with every heartbeat, and the reaper blossoms were four times their usual size and snapped at Maia as she walked by. Cerelia wanted plants that would cause harm to the intruders on their own while Cerelia focused her magic on the vines and thorns that had worked so well against Lord Graves's hunting parties, both at the edge of the woods and then in the garden.

Maia found the witch in the middle of a dense patch of new dragonberry bushes heavy with ripe berries. Cerelia was fashioning additional night fairy traps out of the bushes themselves. When they released the fairies from these traps, they wouldn't be taking them to trade with the gargoyle for eggs.

"I'm ready," Maia announced as she approached. She held up the doll. "It's finished. Now we just need the bloodstone and it will be complete."

Cerelia peered out from between a pair of branches. Her hair was in a thick braid over her shoulder, littered with leaves and a few berries.

Xee crawled from a branch and settled in a twist of Cerelia's braid.

The witch nodded, her face a mix of determination and uncertainty. The branches parted and she came out and took the rampion doll from Maia. "It looks…perfect. I think this would fool a lot of creatures, magical or not."

Maia nodded, suddenly a little choked up. Cerelia sounded proud of her, and she hadn't known how much she'd wanted that.

"This is a good use for that rampion. That stuff has been growing wild ever since you arrived here. It's a good thing you like to eat it. Otherwise, it would have taken over my entire garden, magic or not." Cerelia led the way to the center of the garden.

Maia had been craving the rampion as if her life depended on it, devouring handfuls of it each day. It was as if the baby wanted nothing else, and it made the rampion doll the perfect decoy. She knelt with Cerelia.

"Now, are you really ready?" Cerelia asked.

Nodding, Maia bit her lip. "Yes."

"Let's get you comfortable. I believe that this is going to hurt." Cerelia gestured toward a space that was still more honey clover than rampion.

Trying not to think of the blood that had soaked the garden after Lord Graves's death, Maia kept her eyes on Cerelia as she laid down.

Xee climbed down from Cereliea's braid, down her arm, and hopped onto Maia's belly. Maia watched the spider as it rippled and grew to the size of her hand.

Cerelia knelt next to her and took her hand. "Close your eyes. Think of something beautiful and happy. It will help distract you from the pain."

Maia closed her eyes, Cerelia's hand warm and a little rough over hers. A month ago, she had struggled to trust

Cerelia when she had tied a blindfold over her eyes. Now that Cerelia knew everything about the rumples and Six, Maia was putting the life of her baby in the witch's hands. "Okay, I have my memory. It's my favorite one."

"Tell me about it," Cerelia encouraged.

Maia felt a sharp stab low in her belly. She sucked in a breath.

"Talk to me, Maia. Tell me about your memory. It will help with the pain," Cerelia told her again.

The pain grew stronger. Maia sucked in another breath and let it out. "It was the night you made the Tears of Midnight. They floated in the air like tiny little hopes, and I made a wish on each one."

The pain was so intense that Maia almost forgot what she had been talking about. The memory of the glowing white drops blurred into a streak of milky light.

"What did you wish for? Talk to me, Maia," Cerelia demanded.

"I—" Maia bit her lip, fighting the urge to swat the spider away. Her baby was moving violently inside. She willed herself to remain still and keep her eyes closed until Xee was done extracting the baby's blood. Just one brief moment and it would all be over. "I wished to stay here forever in your garden with you and Xee. I wished to spend the rest of my days trading night fairies for gargoyle eggs and teaching my daughter where the strawberries grow and where the fae foxes hide their young."

Tears flooded her eyes and ran down her cheeks.

A gentle finger wiped them away and Maia realized the pain was fading quickly to a dull ache.

"It's beautiful, Maia. Look." Cerelia's voice sounded reverent.

Maia opened her eyes, her hands instinctively wrapped over her belly.

A small red stone rested in the palm of Cerelia's hand, and Xee was climbing back up to the woman's shoulder. Cerelia helped Maia sit up.

Maia held out her hand. "May I?"

Cerelia nodded and set it in her open palm.

Holding the stone, Maia held her breath. The stone was a deep red with both lighter and darker lines running through it. A stone of her child's blood. It appeared very delicate, as if it would shatter into a million pieces at the touch of a finger.

And Maia could *feel* her daughter in the bloodstone, the bright spirit that was already strong and ready to fight inside her.

"I know why they want her," Maia suddenly thought of the rumple she had seen in the woods. "I saw one, the day I went out to collect the strawberries for you. He was in the shadows of the trees, half-buried by the leaves of a fern. He couldn't move. The night fairies had carved pockets out of his flesh for their young."

"Balance." Cerelia curled Maia's fingers around the stone. "It is the nature of things. We are all predators and we all have our prey, just like the gargoyle eats the night fairies and the night fairies feed on the rumple goblins."

"And the rumple goblins feed on our children," Maia finished.

"Not this time, Maia. We're going to fight them with everything we have," Cerelia promised. "Now, watch."

Maia let Cerelia help her to her feet. Her belly hurt where Xee had stabbed her with her proboscis to draw her baby's blood, but the ache was fading quickly and the baby moved inside her, healthy and strong.

The garden around them had become more menacing than enchanting. Maia shuddered at what was coming.

The vines that Cerelia loved so much and commanded so

easily twisted up from the center of the garden. They wove in and around themselves as they formed a cradle.

A hive fairy fluttered by, its wings flashing a brilliant gold in the sunshine. It dropped a little rose from the bony rose bush into the cradle. Another fairy fluttered by and dropped a fairy bell into the cradle. More fairies followed until the groove of the cradle was covered in a thousand tiny blossoms.

Maia laid the rampion baby inside on the bed of petals, watching the little bloodstone flash a brilliant red in the sun.

15

WHERE THE SPIRIT GOES

Cerelia pinched the bugaboo in her fingers while Xee extracted a drop of blood. The creature squirmed, it's ladybug-like glamour flickering while the spider pierced it.

The bloodstone from the bugaboo was tiny compared to that of Maia's unborn infant, like a red drop of crystal rain. The idea to draw bloodstones had come to Cerelia the last night she had tried to cross beyond the hedge that marked the boundaries of her garden. After she had caught her breath and the pain had gone, she had looked at the garden that had protected her for over a hundred years. It had been her sanctuary and her prison.

Finally, with Maia's arrival, it had become her home.

For years she had kept herself occupied with her plants, moving them around and making new ones. It had become her language, so familiar that she had forgotten how much of it was magical until that wonder had been reflected in Maia's eyes.

Switching the plants was easy when she knew everything about them. Doing the same thing to a living creature had proven to be much more difficult. It wasn't like the orderly formula of stalks and leaves. Each drop of blood had its own signature, its own identity even within the same creature.

But it had a singular scent. That's why she hoped the rumples would fall for the decoy baby.

She had done everything she could to set the garden up to become a war zone when the rumples arrived. The garden had fed on the blood left behind by Six when Maia cut his arm. The reaper blossoms would go rabid as soon as the goblin set foot in the garden. The traps would hold a hundred night fairies who would come to feast on the dragonberries she had forced to ripen.

The reaper blossoms were hungry for goblin blood, and the vines were ready with thorns.

She was ready...almost. She had one more spell to figure out, for the true battle with the rumple goblins was not going to be waged in her garden but in the realm of magic.

Xee settled on her shoulder. With the bugaboo in one hand, she dropped the tiny bloodstone in a doll made of leaves and tender vines much like the rampion doll Maia had made for the baby decoy. Cerelia sat on the ground, connecting to the earth and the source of life for every creature in the forest.

She closed her eyes, gathering the energy.

Blessed be by the law of three;
I gave my heart so this magic may be.
One beat for yesterday, the hour gone by.
One beat for today when the hour is nigh.
One beat for tomorrow with hours unknown
As the essence of one becomes the essence of the other,
For where the spirit goes, the flesh must follow.

The bugaboo squirmed more insistently. If they had teeth

like the night fairies, Cerelia never would have been able to even get through the spell. But the little bugaboo was made for granting children's innocent wishes and fed on nectar and drank water from the spring.

The ladybug shell that the creature appeared to have shifted to wrinkled, doughy flesh, like a smaller version of a night fairy that had wings like a beetle instead of a butterfly.

"Blessed be by the law of three; I gave my heart so this magic may be." She felt the vines move and opened her eyes. The woven shape in her hand changed, becoming more solid.

"One beat for yesterday, the hour gone by. One beat for today when the hour is nigh."

The bugaboo had gone limp, its eyes closed and the glamour completely gone. Now it was the little hairless creature of its true form. It had a disproportionately large round head with creased holes for ears and a plump body with stubby limbs and a hump beneath the shell of its wings.

Within the vine doll, the tiny bloodstone beat once, then again, the rhythm irregular. The vines flattened and widened, connecting to each other and creating a semi-solid form.

"One beat for tomorrow with hours unknown…"

While the little body of the bugaboo was completely still, warm only where Cerelia's hand gave it warmth, the form of the vine doll was growing more solid, the vines changing to a fleshy hue and the head gaining the round shape of the bugaboo, a pair of eyes hollowed out in the middle. Cerelia could still see the bloodstone beating inside, the crystal darkening to the deep, vivid red of living blood.

"As the essence of one becomes the essence of the other, for where the spirit goes, the flesh must follow!" She repeated it over and over again, watching as the vine doll filled in with flesh.

Then the eyes blinked at her. Once. It tried to take a

breath, but the chest was still hollow, the bloodstone heart struggling to beat. The original bugaboo body felt hollow in Cerelia's hand, the creature's soul gone from that side but not completely attached to the new body.

A tiny sound escaped the mouth that had formed in the skull, perhaps a cry or a plea. Cerelia caught it between the syllables of the spell.

And the vine bugaboo's eyes widened, dark and full of fear, and then went as limp as the original.

No…

"Blessed be by the law of three! I gave my heart so this magic may be!" Cerelia chanted.

The little bloodstone remained dark.

"One beat for yesterday, the hour gone by. One beat for today when the hour is nigh," she continued, not ready to give up hope. "One beat for tomorrow with hours unknown…."

There was no change, no movement.

"The essence of one becomes the essence of the other, for where the spirit goes the flesh must follow!" Cerelia chanted the spell a couple more times, willing the new bugaboo to open its eyes and take a breath.

But it was useless. The creature was dead.

She looked back and forth between the little bodies, both dead and one only half-formed. The bloodstone was still and dark.

She was close, so close. The hope in Maia's eyes when she asked for her help dug down in Cerelia's gut and spurred her on. She just needed to try again.

The moon would be full in two days, and she was running out of time. Maia's rumple mark was a dark black and had started to itch.

Cerelia took the two little bugaboo bodies behind the cottage where she had changed the goblin's cap gourd vines to a carnivorous black flower that spit acid. The blossoms looked like eggplants with teeth, whispering at her as she walked by.

She spoke to them quietly and they moved, revealing a small pit where the gargoyle dropped her night fairy bones from the roof. Cerelia had nearly filled it with bugaboo corpses.

Laying the bugaboo and its vine doll twin down, she watched as a root climbed up from the dirt and slid through the two fresh bodies. The pit was nearly full now, the other bugaboos and their vine twins half-rotted back to the earth. She had asked the garden to take them back, to give them peace for the sacrifice they had made.

A worm crawled through the eye of one little corpse, and a potato bug crawled over another. A swarm of centipedes climbed around more of them, their little legs making the pile of dead bugaboos almost look like it was moving.

Cerelia wiped a tear from her cheek as the black flower vines concealed the pit of the dead once more. She took a few more steps to a miniature version of a night fairy trap, this one full of the little ladybug-like bugaboos.

There were five of them left. She plucked a handful of tender vines and started weaving another doll.

16

A DESPERATE PLEA

Maia stood next to the cradle of vines and brushed her fingers over the baby made of rampion. The bloodstone was darker beneath the moonlight, smooth flashes of red peeping through the woven onion stalks.

It was the final full moon. They had been waiting for the baby to come. The garden was ready, although Cerelia walked the border of the hedge wall several times a day and checked on each of her plants. She was restless enough for both of them.

Maia had felt surprisingly calm. She had spent her days out in the sun of the garden, feeling the baby move and thinking about the life she had lived in the handful of months since she had escaped Lord Graves and his minions.

That morning, the baby had shifted, sitting lower inside and hardly moving at all, and the rumple mark had started to itch and burn.

It was time.

Cerelia came up behind her.

"It's a beautiful cradle," Maia said. "Thank you."

Xee crawled over the vines that created the edge of the cradle, stopping to raise her front legs as if she had caught a scent in the air.

"It will hold your baby soon. You're real baby." Cerelia tried to give her a comforting look, but it was twisted with fear.

Maia gave her a sad smile, weighed down by the looming reality of the situation. "Promise me something, Cerelia."

Cerelia nodded. "Anything."

"Promise me that you will save her. No matter what it costs. Let the rumples take me, but save her." Maia held her hands over her belly, the baby still.

"I promise I will save you both. We are ready for them, all of us in the garden. The reaper blossoms and the burrs and the thorns on the vines. When they come, hide in the cottage and I will take care of the rumples. They will die a quick death at my hands, or they can suffer their fate at the mercy of the night fairies." Cerelia put a hand on Maia's shoulder.

Maia hesitated, studying the shape of the rampion doll on the flower blanket, the little head and arms and legs. Xee had crawled inside the rampion shell and sat on the bloodstone, the white of her body a stark contrast to the deep red. For a moment, the spider looked like she was made of moonlight.

"They will suffer," Maia finally agreed, letting Cerelia have her hopes of truly defeating the rumples while Maia had accepted some of the reality of the situation.

Even though the fight would take place in Cerelia's garden, the rumples definitely had the upper hand. They'd had the upper hand since the moment Maia signed the contract with Six. The magic was clearly on the rumples' side, and Cerelia and Maia had not found a way around that.

Now Maia only hoped that Cerelia could somehow protect her baby, and it was only a matter of hours before they would know. The itch of the rumple mark on Maia's arm was starting to grow warm, almost painful.

Maia sat on the grass, her back against the cradle. Cerelia sat next to her, the two of them looking at the moon and the stars.

Taking Cerelia's hand, Maia swallowed her tears. More pooled in her eyes and ran down her cheeks. She thought of Doni and Catherine, the way they had given in to their fear of Lord Graves and their hatred of the unknown. The way they had been willing to sacrifice her life at the slightest threat.

But Cerelia had been everything Maia had ever wanted in a mother, and Maia needed her to know that before she lost her chance to tell her. As she spoke, she managed to keep her voice steady. "Thank you for giving me the happiest days of my life. You have been more of a mother to me in these few months than all the others who ever took me in. You shared your life and your magic with me. Without that, I would have died in these woods never having known what it meant to be loved."

Cerelia squeezed her hand. Maia looked at the woman, noticing the lines of exhaustion that pulled at her eyes.

"You are my daughter, Maia. Not by blood, but by soul. You have become quite a warrior. You gave Lord Graves exactly what he deserved, and Six will not take us lightly when it is time. Ah, brave girl, we could still have a happy ending." Tears threatened in Cerelia's eyes.

Maia fought her own tears. "A warrior, but not a witch."

Cerelia shook her head, then wrapped her arm around Maia's shoulders. Her next words sent chills down Maia's spine rather than comfort. "Not yet, dear girl."

Maia leaned her head on Cerelia's shoulder. She had been on guard for so long now that it was taking its toll, and she was tired. She plucked a rampion stalk from the ground and twisted it in her fingers. "I want you to teach her to be as strong as you."

Cerelia laughed through her tears. "Even better. I promise I will teach her to be as strong as you."

Maia didn't argue, although she didn't think of accepting defeat as being strong. She knew the rumple goblins would take her life. She couldn't think of a way around that. There had to be some balance.

After a moment of silence, Cerelia spoke again. "There was a lullaby that my mother sung to me when I was small. It's the only thing I still remember of her."

Maia closed her eyes. With Cerelia next to her, she felt the safest she ever had. Not just safe, but wanted. For the first time in Maia's life, with the threat of the rumples looming and the garden battle-ready, she felt like she truly belonged. She sensed the protective affection of the reaper blossoms which she had fed bugaboos, the watchful eye of Septaria on the roof of the cottage, and the soft caress of the honey clover on her ankles as she sat with Cerelia in the heart of the garden.

She was home.

Cerelia sang. Maia heard the song as it vibrated through Cerelia's body as well as hearing it carry through the night air. The melody was both soothing and haunting, a promise and a warning at once.

Hush now, darling; close your eyes,
Dream yourself a thousand lives.
One life of true love; one life of power;
One life of kissing crows in a witch's crumbling tower.
One life on a pirate ship with chests full of gold,
And one life in a land where you'll never grow old.
Sleep now, darling; close your eyes.
Dream of a world with no goodbyes.

Maia wasn't sure how long she had been sleeping. The moon was high overhead and the stars dotted the clear sky.

The mark on her arm had started to burn. Pressure wrapped around her lower back, pulling at her like a rope was squeezing around her waist.

Next to her, Cerelia still had her eyes on the moon. The woman hadn't moved a leaf's breadth since Maia had fallen asleep to the lullaby.

"Cerelia." She sat up.

Cerelia looked at Maia's arm. The rumple mark was glowing a bright gold. "They're coming."

"So is the baby," Maia exhaled as the pressure increased. "It must be like a beacon. The mark burned when I called them like it's burning now."

"Get inside. Xee will protect you." Cerelia helped Maia to her feet. "Go!"

Xee rode on Maia's shoulder as she walked slowly toward the cottage. Once inside, she checked the hatchet and a dozen giant thorns that Cerelia had made for her to use as spears in the event that the rumples made it past the plants and the night fairies.

The vines of the cottage wall opened up. Maia grabbed the hatchet and slipped inside, then the vines closed over her, creating a cocoon lit by the glow of three vine orbs.

Maia gripped the handle of the hatchet. The burn of the rumple mark hurt far more than the contractions, but they were getting stronger quickly. Xee was nowhere to be seen inside the vine cocoon. The spider must have jumped off her shoulder before the vines closed her in.

The ground shook. She heard the muffled sounds of yelling and destruction.

She took a deep breath and waited.

17

WHILE THE MOON IS NIGH

Cerelia watched as Maia slipped inside the cottage. The rumple mark that Maia had sewn onto the slip of fabric gave off a faint golden glow from within the rampion doll.

The decoy was working. Cerelia did not expect that it would be enough to completely fool the rumples, but she hoped it would give her a few moments to attack first once they had arrived.

She knelt down and placed her hands on the ground, listening to the plants whisper about the rumple goblins who were coming. The plants sensed the connection between the goblins and the magic of the rumple mark that was their beacon, drawing them to the unborn child and Cerelia's garden.

From what Cerelia could gather, the rumple goblins traveled on the edge of the physical realm, the plants picking up the subtle vibrations of their passing. They were traveling fast, coming from somewhere deep in the enchanted forest.

The night fairies grew restless, scratching and biting at the vine cages that Cerelia had made to hold them. She had trapped them drunk on dragonberries and let them go hungry for the past few days while she and Maia had waited for the goblins to come.

They started to hiss and fight with each other. Cerelia heard it through the whispers of the vines as well as her own ears.

She sent thin tendrils of magic throughout the garden, waking the burrs and the reaper blossoms and thorned vine shoots along the boundary of the garden. As they had seen when Maia chopped into Six's arm, once the goblins materialized, they were bound to the physical laws of this dimension. They could be killed like anything else made of flesh.

Let them come. She was ready.

The night fairies' restlessness rose in a sharp crescendo, the little creatures going rabid inside their cages.

Cerelia stood. She felt a focused rush of air and a shimmer as if space and time were bending.

The rampion doll was gone. The bloodstone sat on the blanket of flowers that lined the vine nest of the cradle, its dark red center glowing as if it were absorbing the moonlight. It had fallen out of its rampion shell.

Six's words echoed in her memory. *It is the gift of the mother that holds the magic.*

The bloodstone had not been the decoy at all. It had been only the rumple mark that they used to track their prey.

Opening the twist of vines that formed the support of the cradle, Cerelia climbed inside the space beneath it and closed the vines behind her. She could feel her heart beating in the ground beneath her, and she heard the whispers of all the plants in the garden.

They are here. They are here. They are here.

She held her hands to the earth, ready.

The clamoring of the night fairies was deafening.

Then she heard a chuckle, a deep morbid cackling that sent shivers down her spine.

"Mortal, mortal…"

Six.

She smelled the fire before she saw the flames, tendrils of thick, green smoke choking her in her space inside the vines. Then the flames peeked through, flickering red fingers that clawed their way toward her.

Cerelia shared the plants' pain as the fire took hold.

"Here I be," Six continued, the final syllable drawn out into a dark warning.

The smoke stung her eyes and she muffled a cough.

"Come out and play with me, witch." The goblin's voice was eerily close.

A clawed hand ripped through the vines that were burning down around Cerelia.

She broke free from her enclosure beneath the cradle, the vines fluttering to the ground in burning ash.

She released the night fairies, bursting open their dragonberry cages. They swarmed a giant rumple goblin that was tearing thatch out of the cottage roof. Cerelia charged the vines that had climbed the hedge wall and they grew giant thorns as long as her arms. A thorn caught one goblin through the neck and another in the thigh.

She looked around the garden, counting at least half a dozen more rumple goblins in their red hats. These were twice the size of Six, beefy goblin soldiers with glowing eyes that matched the red of their caps.

The fairies had taken down one goblin, swarming over him in such a thick cloud of wings and teeth that the only part of him Cerelia could make out was the red cap. The goblin's scream faded into a garbled plea for help.

She heard the snap of a reaper blossom and a goblin cry.

Septaria clawed at another goblin tearing thatch from the

roof, raking through both red eyes. The goblin hardly seemed deterred, trying to find a way inside past the thorns that riddled the cottage walls.

But even though Six had been taunting her while she hid, Cerelia didn't see him anywhere in her garden.

He was going for Maia. The rampion doll and the bloodstone had only worked for a second, but at least it had been enough time for Cerelia to activate the defenses of the garden.

And it was working, mostly. There were more goblins than she had expected. The plants were fighting just as she'd hoped, and the night fairies had a second goblin paralyzed beneath their swarm.

Their attempts to negotiate with Six had only tipped the goblins off that they would be coming to a battle when they came to collect Maia's baby.

But still she couldn't find Six. He was the one who mattered.

The one she had to kill.

A goblin tore at the door to the cottage, three long thorns piercing through the ribs on its side. Blood ran down in thick streams, but the goblin didn't even seem to notice.

Cerelia looked at the others that had been injured. They were all back in the fight, limping and bleeding but searching for Maia with frightening persistence. It was as if they didn't feel pain. The only two that had been truly defeated had been those taken down by the night fairies.

The goblin that had been pierced in the neck by the vine wall had pulled the thorn out and lumbered toward the cottage. The reaper blossoms had chewed off the leg of another and he was pulling himself toward the cottage with arms, dragging his other leg which was now missing a foot.

She rushed toward the cottage as the goblin on the roof caught Septaria's leg in his long fingers. He swung the creature around and smashed her against the cottage wall. A thorn pierced through the gargoyle's chest and throat. She thrashed, her wings beating the air, but she couldn't free herself. A goblin had joined another on the roof. After a few handfuls of thatch and vines, they fell through inside the cabin.

The goblin at the door had torn it off.

Before she could make it to the cottage, Six materialized right in front of her out of a shimmer of the night air. He held the rampion doll wedged against his body beneath the arm that Maia had chopped into. The limb fell limp beneath the elbow, useless.

"How entertaining you have made our collecting on this full moon. Thank you for such a grand welcome. Humans are interesting creatures of hope, despite how limited and frail you are. You knew you did not have even a sliver of a chance in this realm in defeating my magic and yet you still tried." He grinned, his sharp teeth gleaming in the moonlight. He held up his good hand and stretched out long, curved claws.

Cerelia took a step back, her eyes flitting around the garden, trying to decide how to get past Six and to the cottage before the rumples found Maia's hiding place.

The flames devouring the cradle had grown tall, their light flickering behind her and dancing across Six's cruel, stretched face.

A dozen night fairies fluttered around the goblin, looking at him strangely as they sniffed and flew away.

"It's not over yet, Six. I will fight until all of you are dead and your corpses are worm fodder." Cerelia took another step back as Six got closer.

"It was over the moment the girl signed the contract, my dear witch. There is no magic in this world that can keep me from collecting the child, and certainly not green magic as petty and restricted as yours." Six twisted his head around to look behind him at the destruction of the cottage. "Do not worry. They will not harm her until the child is born and the contract fulfilled. Then she will no longer matter, will she?"

"She will always matter, you ancient bastard of magic." Cerelia glared at Six when he turned back to face her again. "Take her baby and she will destroy you. A witch is born when from her is torn something greater than her soul. You made your contract too early. You gave her time to love her child and now it is you who is tempting your fate against a greater magic."

Six grinned. "Then I supposed she'll have to die."

The words chilled Cerelia and she fought a surge of panic. She couldn't give in to her fear or Maia and the baby would be lost.

Xee burst out from inside the cottage, a goblin hanging from her pincers. The spider scattered thatch and vine scraps everywhere. The gargoyle landed limply in the midst of the dragonberry bushes, her wings torn from thrashing against the long thorns that protruded from the cottage walls.

Xee tossed the goblin over the vine wall that surrounded the garden and pierced another with a leg. Another goblin had made it under Xee's belly and started to tear at the vine cocoon that held Maia.

Flames spread from the cradle and out into the garden. They licked at the demon fruit trees and bit into the reaper blossoms, burning right over the honey clover and the fairy bells.

Cerelia felt it all as if it were her own flesh that was burning.

She wrapped a vine around Six's ankle, holding the goblin in place while she charged past him. She only made it a few steps before she was frozen in place, her feet no longer on the ground.

It was a full breath later that the pain—her own pain and not that of her garden or her spider—burst through her body like lightning. She looked down at Six's claws going into her ribs on one side of her body and the sharp little tips poking out on the other side.

She screamed.

18

ONE BEAT FOR FOREVER

Cerelia's scream rippled through every living thing in the garden and straight into Maia's heart.

"No, please. No, she can't die. Not because of me." Maia chopped at her enclosure with the hatchet. The space was too small for her to get a good hard swing, but that did little to deter her.

A contraction hit. Hard. She doubled over. She held onto a vine, squeezing as hard as she could while the pressure from her lower back wrapped up around her belly and she couldn't breathe for a moment.

The rumple mark on her arm burned.

She was running out of time.

The entire cottage rumbled, the vine walls shaking so hard that Maia had to hold on to the wall to keep herself on her feet. Thatch from the roof fell like snow into her hair and drifted to the floor.

Smoke followed, filling in the space.

Between that and the next contraction, Maia struggled to swing the hatchet. She brought it up, as far overhead as she could manage, ready to bring it down with her full strength.

Then the vines tore away from the other side and she was face to face with a large, angry goblin. Two giant thorns pierced his neck and one stuck out from his ribcage. Blood streamed down from the wounds, but the goblin didn't look like he even noticed them more than he would have paid attention to a sliver in his finger.

With a yell, Maia brought the hatchet forward. The blade landed between the goblin's eyes, sinking inches deep into his skull. His eyes rolled back and he slumped to the ground, his leathery skin folding over the width of his shoulders. Blood pooled beneath him, making the ground slick as Maia fought to free her weapon.

Outside of the cocoon, the world had become a violent storm of destruction. Xee had grown to the size of the cottage, which was almost completely destroyed. Fire licked at the dragonberries and climbed the hedge wall that surrounded the garden.

Night fairies swarmed around two of the goblins, screeching joyfully as they carved hollows out of their guts. A few of them flew over to where Maia had just managed to free her hatchet from the dead goblin's skull. The fairies sniffed at the blood and flew away.

That goblin was dead.

Xee picked up a goblin in her pincers and threw it out into the moonlit night. Even above the crackle of the growing fire and the excited noises of the night fairies, Maia heard the goblin thump against a tree.

She hovered behind the spider for a moment, scanning the garden for Cerelia. The fire blazed high over the cradle Cerelia had made for the rampion doll, the flames licking at the night sky.

And there, in the fire's hungry flickering glow, she saw Cerelia. Her dark braid fell over one shoulder, framing eyes wide with pain and shock.

Six stood next to her, an evil grin on his face.

Then Maia made out the blood on Cerelia's dress where Six's claws went clear through her ribcage.

Another contraction hit and the rumple mark burned like hot iron against her flesh. Maia fell to her knees on top of the goblin she had just killed, her weight supported by the hatchet. She breathed hard, grunting as the pain momentarily consumed her.

As the pressure ebbed, she looked back over to Six and Cerelia. The rumple goblin looked small compared to the one she had just killed and the others that had fallen to the night fairies. Cerelia was at least a head taller than the gnarled little man. Maia hadn't noticed until they were standing so close to each other. Six was smaller, but far, far more dangerous than anything else Maia had ever heard of in any fairy tale.

Xee let out a screech that rang in Maia's ears more than it made any sound. She flinched as the spider's head fell forward, a pair of goblins hanging from her pincers. Another tore at her front leg and she buckled on that side.

Three more goblins shimmered out of the flame-lit darkness.

Maia looked back over at Six and Cerelia. She met the goblin's dark eyes, an evil, satisfied smirk on his face.

Cerelia turned her head toward Maia. She opened her mouth as if to speak, but all that came out was a bubble of blood that popped between her lips and then dripped down her chin.

Six grinned at Maia and jerked his arm away from Cerelia.

Time slowed. The sounds around Maia dulled to a faint roar.

The crackle of the hungry flames.

Xee's otherworldly cry of pain.

The growls of the giant rumple goblins as they fought the giant spider.

The gleeful chattering of the night fairies…

And her own scream as Cerelia fell to the ground.

Maia struggled to her feet, leveraging one foot against the goblin's head to pull out the hatchet. A gush of water ran down her leg, mixing with the goblin's blood as she stepped over him and stumbled toward the center of the garden where Six waited for her next to Cerelia.

Cerelia.

Maia couldn't believe she was dead. Cerelia couldn't be dead. She was a witch, Maia's everything, her only hope for the life inside her.

She dragged the hatchet across the garden, stepping over crushed burrs and torn up reaper blossoms. She gathered a strange comfort from the goblin limbs she saw half-chewed or burned among the destroyed plants and the goblins paralyzed and suffering as the night fairies laid their eggs inside of them.

The pain of the rumple mark flared and another contraction hit. Maia closed her eyes for a brief moment and begged her body to give her more time.

The contraction ebbed.

She raised the hatchet and charged at Six.

"Mortal, mortal, here I be," Six said.

Maia stumbled halfway between where the cottage had stood and Cerelia's limp form. She caught herself on her knees again, her arm a blaze of heat and pain.

"Come to hear your desperate plea," Six continued, taking a small step toward Maia.

The pain in her arm was so intense that the next contraction was nothing but an echo of that pain.

"Blood for blood will end your plight," Six grinned, his sharp teeth needles of hatred between his thin lips.

Maia looked away from the goblin, her eyes on Cerelia's dark hair and pale hands. The blood pooling beneath the witch shimmered in the light of the flames.

A few more feet…

"Signed by soul this curs-ed night," Six finished, stepping close to Maia as she collapsed next to Cerelia.

The woman was as pale as the moonlight, her dark lashes brushing against her cheeks. Her braid wound around her throat like a noose, the holes through her dress from Six's claws gaping slightly as Cerelia sucked in shallow breaths.

But she was *breathing*.

She was alive.

The goblins hadn't won yet.

Maia brushed a finger along Cerelia's cheekbone. "I'm here. Open your eyes. Please."

Cerelia's eyes fluttered open. They looked strange, the pupils swallowing her irises as if she didn't see Maia at all but was looking into another dimension.

She placed her hand over Maia's.

Then her eyes closed again, and she went limp.

"Cerelia!" Maia fought the urge to give in to the pain in her own body. She choked on the thick smoke from the burning green things.

Six's shadow fell over them, the light from the fire behind him casting its shadow over his face.

Maia shook Cerelia. "Call the garden. Let it take you, please. You'll be okay. Like you were after Lord Graves's sword."

Cerelia did not open her eyes. Her hand slipped down to the ground, her fingers nearly lost in the thick, dark pool of blood beneath her.

"No, please," Maia started to sob, her tears cut short as she was lost in the pain of the rumple mark and another contraction.

The ground moved beneath her, a subtle slithering that tickled Maia's ankles and wrists.

It was happening. Cerelia was speaking to the vines, letting them take her.

Maia nearly passed out with the relief. Cerelia would live.

Then the vines twisted and tightened around *her*, sliding up her legs and arms and wrapping around her.

"No, not me. Cerelia, please. Save yourself. Do not let them have her. Please." She fought to be free. "You're the only one who can save us."

The vines grew thicker and faster, covering half of Maia in a matter of heartbeats.

"Blood for blood! She is mine!" Six tore at the vines with his claws, tearing them from Maia and cutting her in the process. Her dress hung in tatters as Six dragged her away from Cerelia's limp body.

"No!" Maia screamed, the sound cut short when a contraction took hold of her.

Six couldn't pick her up, his right arm nothing more than a shriveled appendage below the elbow where Maia had almost chopped it off with the hatchet. Another rumple goblin picked her up in his arms, cradling her like a baby. She pinched and kicked, but it was as if he didn't even feel her through his thick skin.

The rumple followed Six through a section of the vine wall where the fire had burned a hole through it, and he carried her into the trees where the moonlight only shone through in shards between the leaves.

Dizzy with pain, Maia glanced over the goblin's shoulder at the devastation behind them. The vine wall was melted in places where the fire had eaten through, leaving irregular, charred windows that looked in on the garden.

The cottage was a tall blaze beside Xee's motionless and lopsided body, her head and front legs smashed into pieces of white exoskeleton. The cradle that Cerelia had made for the rampion doll was a charred lump now, Cerelia's body beside it.

As the pain of a contraction came and went, the edges of Maia's vision closed in and her only awareness was of the jolting of the goblin's steps between the sharp crescendos of pain.

19

BY BLOOD, BRAIN, MEAT, AND BONE

Cerelia's eyes blinked open and focused on a slender piece of grass in front of her face.

No, not grass. A rampion stalk. Firelight flickered along its height, giving it a sharp edge that danced with the flame.

Fire.

Rumples.

Maia.

Cerelia tried to sit up, pushing herself up on her hands. Pain sliced through her torso and she couldn't breathe. The world spun. She closed her eyes.

It took her a moment to take in a single shallow breath. Then another. Then she coughed at the smoke that hovered over the garden and nearly passed out from the pain the motion brought on.

Once she had taken a few more shallow breaths, she opened her eyes.

The garden was destroyed. Everything she had known, nurtured, and cared about was burned or crushed. The cottage was a heap of smoking ashes, half of it under Xee's twisted body. Cerelia could tell by the angle of the spider's corpse that she was dead, half of one leg lying a few feet away from the giant white abdomen.

She sent out a silent call to her familiar. Her mind searched the void between worlds for the spider's essence, the void where only the two of them existed. She found nothing but a complete and endless emptiness.

Grief for the spider washed over her in a wave. Xee had been her only companion for more years than most human lifetimes, her only connection to the world outside. Her chest tightened, a new pain making it hard to breathe. She felt the grief of the entire garden.

New blood ran from her wounds where Six had stabbed her through with his claws.

Night fairies fluttered around two different goblin bodies that lay on opposite sides of the garden, one by the reaper blossoms and the other half hidden in the scorched dragonberry bushes. The reaper blossoms had been stomped into a black and red mash, but not before they had torn off at least one goblin's leg.

The vine and hedge wall was honeycombed with holes burned through by the fire that was still hanging on parts of it. Beyond the garden, the forest looked untouched, the thick late summer leaves of the trees silhouetted against the fading moonlight.

And beside her, the cradle with the doll was a lump of ash.

Cerelia turned onto her hands and knees, waiting again until the pain settled enough that the world stopped spinning. She needed to let the earth take her, to heal, but there was no time.

Maia and the baby would be dead by then. If there was even still time now.

Memories from the night she herself had run away from

home flashed through her mind. The baying of the hounds. The blood running down her legs. The deep betrayal that had nearly destroyed her soul.

Her baby had been the only reason she had made it as far as she had. And this is where the forest had given her a home. Where her heart still beat beneath the ash and the blood.

This had been Maia's first true home, too. Cerelia thought of the night the girl had stumbled into the garden, the night she had seen the deer.

The forest had warned her what was coming.

The hatchet sat nearby, the blade covered in dried black blood.

Goblin blood.

Cerelia curled her fingers around the wooden handle, pride making its way through her devastation.

Maia had become a warrior.

Crawling a few feet and dragging the hatchet along in one sticky hand, Cerelia made it to what was left of the vine cradle. A few leaves were untouched, still thick and green, while others were nothing but once-living outlines made of ash. Hot, tiny fingers of flame still caressed the gray bark.

Cerelia sifted through the debris, looking for the baby's bloodstone. The spell she had tried on the bugaboos was far from perfect, but it was all she could think to try. Even if she weren't injured and weak from loss of blood, she couldn't leave the garden to chase after Maia, not that she had any idea where the rumple goblins had taken her.

This was the cost for all the years the garden had protected her. It had also become her prison.

Cerelia sat back on her heels, almost too weak to stay upright. Her hands were sticky with blood, her side soaked through where the blood had pooled beneath her in the grass.

She needed more onion stalks. What had been growing around the cradle had been burned.

Careful to distribute what little strength she had, she drew tendrils of magic from beneath the earth where her heart beat, and she grew a new patch of the onions that Maia had craved for the past few months.

She wiped the blood from her hands on the new rampion stalks and plucked them from the ground.

"Blessed be by the law of three, I gave my heart so this magic may be." She wove as she chanted, forming the rest of the baby's body. She fleshed out the torso, then the arms and legs. It was a perfect little body, covered in her blood and heavier than she would have expected from something hollow.

But it was full of the life of the garden, the magic and the love that had protected Cerelia for a century running through the plump stalks.

"One beat for yesterday, the hour gone by. One beat for tonight while the moon is nigh."

Cradling the rampion doll in her arms, she watched as the bloodstone started to glow. It ignited a small seed of hope.

"By blood, brain, meat, and bone…"

A breeze picked up in the garden, blowing the smoke away and carrying whispers.

"The essence of the unborn…"

The bloodstone grew brighter. Over one shoulder of the doll, the striated green stalks of the rampion smoothed out and faded to a flesh tone, pale in the moonlight.

"…becomes the essence known."

The rampion smoothed to flesh down one arm, extending to a set of tiny fingers. The face started to fill in and flesh out around a hollow for an eye. A set of lips plumped out and a dimple formed in the chin.

"One beat for forever, my wishes bestow."

The bloodstone glowed like a red star inside its rampion shell, more of the onion stalks turning to flesh and blood.

"For where the spirit goes, the flesh must follow."

An eye began to form, then the mouth moved.

Cerelia chanted louder, the edges of her vision going dark. The little soul was only halfway into this world. She could sense the pain that Maia was in, the fear and anger that seethed within her even as she was giving birth to her daughter, a magical connection to them through the bloodstone.

So much fear and anger.

Cerelia begged Maia to fight with her.

She forced her eyes open. She had fallen over, her arm slung across the half-burned cradle and her wounds bleeding mercilessly.

I think that you are even more powerful than you believe, Cerelia. Your love has saved us all, even you.

More powerful than she believed. But only while her heart fed her magic.

Her heart.

Cerelia cradled the rampion doll in one arm. The flesh that had started to form had withered and blown away like flakes of brittle paper. It was nothing but onion stalks again, with the bloodstone glowing faintly inside.

She could try the spell again and again. She was not giving up, even if it cost her immortality. She placed her hand to the ground and drew on the life of the garden, on her heart. Below the ground, nothing had been burnt. It was merely waiting for the smoke and embers to die to surface again beneath the moonlight.

She leaned into the rhythm of her heartbeat. It was strong, determined.

I think that you are more powerful than you believe.

She chanted the spell. The bloodstone glowed brighter.

The flesh reformed over the rampion doll's shoulder, down one arm, formed an eye.

It blinked.

It was working.

Cerelia chanted louder, the magic stirring up the night air. She choked on the ash, but still she continued to chant.

> *Blessed be by the law of three,*
> *I gave my heart so this magic may be.*
> *One beat for yesterday, the hour gone by.*
> *One beat for tonight while the moon is nigh.*
> *By blood, brain, meat, and bone,*
> *The essence of the unborn becomes the essence known.*
> *One beat for forever, my wishes bestow,*
> *For where the spirit goes, the flesh must follow.*

A loud crack rent the air. The air stilled and the ash floated to the ground. Cerelia looked at the half-formed infant in her arm, still and dark. The bloodstone had split in half.

She slumped back, sitting on her heels and then sliding to lean against the remains of the cradle. The weight of her hip settled on something hard. She pulled it out from under her.

It was the hatchet.

Her heartbeat quickened and the rhythm carrying up through the earth stirred her blood.

Setting the rampion doll carefully to the side, Cerelia stumbled to her feet and picked up the hatchet.

And she swung at the ground.

SIGNED BY SOUL

Through a haze of pain, Maia made out the flicker of torchlight along the rough arch of cave walls. She remembered being carried by a large rumple goblin through the forest, screaming as loud as she could to be set free, to let her baby live. That must have been less than an hour ago, but with each contraction, everything else in the world drifted further and further away.

The rumple mark on her arm had reached a level of pain that Maia no longer felt it. It was as if her arm had been cut off and discarded. She could see it, covered in dirt and blood and the rumple mark glowing as if it were made of fire itself, but it was as if the arm belonged to some other pregnant girl hugging her round belly.

And more than just the arm felt like it belonged to someone else. Other sensations in the cave felt like they were being experienced by some other part of Maia, too, as if her consciousness had been split, one half observing her from outside her body and the other half trapped inside the haze of fear and pain. While she was hot, the cave felt cool, as if it were somewhere underground. She could smell damp earth, like when she had pulled up a plant by the roots.

She was propped up on several thick furs that had been piled inside a depression in the cave floor. There were no midwife's implements, no bowls of water and rags to cool her forehead, no strips of cloth to tie off the cord and soak up the blood.

No swaddling ready for wrapping the baby once she came.

There were a few strange tools that looked like they belonged to a tanner or a butcher set on a ledge in the stone. Next to those was a bowl carved from a single piece of wood, dark stains rippling through the grain.

This was not the birth of a child. This was the end of a hunt when the hunters prepared for the feast.

Signed by soul.

Maia searched through the haze for Six. There was a rumple goblin standing a few feet from her, one of the big ones who had come to attack the garden and carry her away.

"Six?" she croaked out. Her throat hurt, raw from smoke and fear.

The goblin smiled with its wicked teeth and left the little cave. She didn't know if he would return and she didn't care.

She was alone. If her legs still worked, she could run. At least she had to try.

Gripping the edge of the stone ledge, Maia sat upright. She rolled to her side, trying to get her feet under her enough that she could push herself up.

But that was as far as she could move. She was chained to the wall.

Suddenly she felt as if she were back in Lord Graves's dungeon with the villagers outside chanting for her to burn while she listened to the scurrying of the rats.

A contraction set in. She doubled over. The world went

dark and she lost her sense of place, as if her body was floating in a void and everything she remembered was part of a dream. The burning of the garden. Xee's limp, lopsided body. Cerelia lying next to what remained of the cradle she had made for the rampion doll.

When the pressure faded, the cave came back into a hazy focus. Maia settled herself back on the pile of furs and caught her breath. A bead of sweat dripped over her right temple and down into her eye.

The room was still empty except for her.

"Rumple, rumple, hear my plight. Come to me this cursed night." It came out as little more than a rough whisper.

When she had blinked the sweat out of her eye, Six stood in front of her.

"I believe you called for me?" Six brushed the base of his throat with his long claws. "The time that your child will come into this world is nigh. There is no need for conversation, and the time for negotiation has long ended, not that you were any good at that particular game. Mortals rarely get what they wish when trying to cut a bargain with a magical creature."

"Cerelia?" Maia croaked out. "Is she alive?"

"Alive? She has not had her heartbeat within her body for over a hundred years. I do not know if she can be killed." Six sniffed the air and grinned. "She is connected to you. I can smell her clearly now. Dragonberries and heartbreak. The stuff that witches are made of."

The goblin's words about Cerelia gave Maia hope. The witch could still be alive. She could still come for her, still somehow save her daughter.

Another contraction made the room go dark for a moment. While the edges of her vision blacked out, Maia hovered in a realm between this one and the next.

Somewhere in that space, she heard the faint sound of a woman singing.

Hush now, darling; close your eyes.

Dream yourself a thousand lives.

The contraction and the singing both faded.

Maia looked at Six, a hungry grin on the goblin's face. She reached over and picked up one of the strange tools from the ledge. It looked like a miniature scythe, the curved blade glinting in the torchlight. She held it to her throat. "If I killed myself now, would that pay your blood price? Would you let my baby live?"

Six scowled. "Put that down. You mortals have no sense of honor. You signed that contract with your soul, Maia. No matter what you do, the magic will make sure that it is fulfilled."

Maia dropped the blade as the next contraction started. This time, she felt the baby shift under the pressure. She could feel the rumple mark again, burning low and tingling.

The room dimmed and she heard more singing.

One life of true love; one life of power.

One life of kissing crows in a witch's crumbling tower.

When her vision cleared, she grinned at Six. "A witch is born when from her is torn something greater than her soul."

"That is why there are so few witches." Six clasped his hands in front of him. "The gift of an infant, while valuable to the rumple goblins, does not qualify as something torn. It is willingly gifted and therefore more powerful for our purposes. Despite the way the humans portray us in their tales, we do not steal babies. We pay for them. You already received your part of the blood price. Now you must fulfill your part of the agreement."

"And what if I killed you?" Maia pointed at him and smiled. "What if I slit your throat and watched your blood soak your wrinkled gray skin? Would that pay my blood price?"

The scowl on Six's face deepened. "What you seem to find humorous in this eludes me. I do not see what you seek to gain in addition to the death of the mortal which you asked me to destroy. There is nothing left for you now but to deliver the child to me. Then you may die in whatever peace awaits one such as you."

Another contraction came, this one longer and harder. Maia closed her eyes and listened to the singing. She recognized Cerelia's voice, and realized the words were the lullaby that the older woman had sung to her in the garden while they waited for the goblins to come.

She sang along, her voice echoing the other that she realized Six could not hear. "*One life on a pirate ship with chests full of gold.*"

The baby was coming now. She felt it move with each contraction.

Six saw it, his eyes large and hungry. He hissed and a line of saliva dripped down his chin.

"*And one life in a land where you'll never grow old.*" Maia focused on Cerelia's voice. For a moment, she could see the garden, the night fairies swarming over the fallen rumple goblins, and Xee's body in the middle of the cottage remains.

Then the rough walls of the cave came back into focus. She placed her hands on each side of her, one settling on the handle with the curved blade, and she pushed. Sweat poured down her face and between her breasts. She felt as if she was being torn apart from the inside out.

She kept her eyes on Six.

The goblin watched her with hungry eyes.

A world of summer; a world of play;
A world of wishes and night-cursed fae.

Cerelia's voice carried through the pain. It was the same lullaby, but the lines were new.

Maia could feel the baby leaving her body.

A world where the moon sheds her midnight tears.

And the salt of the sea washes clean our fears.

Six picked up the bowl from the ledge.

Maia gritted her teeth and bore down for the final push.

The baby was out.

Six stared, his face frozen in a strange expression of anger and surprise.

Hush now, darling; don't you cry.

I'll give you the world of the sun and sky.

The voice faded with the last word, and with it ended Mai's connection to the garden. Cerelia had never been singing to her, she had been singing to the baby.

Six held up the little body. It was limp and motionless.

Maia looked more closely.

The baby was a corpse, half-formed flesh intertwined with rampion stalks.

Maia laughed, a deep laugh that bubbled up through the pain and the blood.

Six hovered over her, his face twisted with shock. "What magic is this?"

"Blood for blood. Your contract is complete." Maia continued to laugh.

And then something new replaced the pain. A feeling of power, as if she were full of fire and brimstone. It started deep inside her, an internal sun that expanded and consumed her soul.

"A witch is born…" Maia began.

"No!" Six threw the bowl against the wall of the cave.

Rocks and dust showered down on Maia, dirt filling her mouth. She smiled at the goblin. "…when from her is torn…"

"I tore nothing from you! It was a gift!" Spit flew from

Six's mouth. "You signed a contract. That child belongs to me! I know her scent. I will find her."

Tears ran down Maia's face as she realized this power filling her body was also part of Cerelia's final gift.

Six picked up the tool with the curved blade from the cave shelf. "I cannot stand the sound of human grieving."

Maia beckoned to the goblin to come closer, and then closer still. As clever as he thought he was, Maia found it satisfying that he was not clever enough to understand that he had not torn her child from her, but Cerelia had.

Something greater than her soul. She was now a witch.

And with that transformation came an understanding of how much it would cost Maia to destroy a creature as ancient and powerful as a rumple goblin.

It was a price she would gladly pay.

Six gave her a greedy grin, turning the curved blade over in his good hand.

She beckoned again, holding back the fire inside her.

Not yet.

The goblin stepped closer.

Maia beckoned again.

He leaned over, his face close enough for Maia to smell the rot that slimed his sharp, needle-like teeth.

"Tears come from pain and grief, but they can also come from joy." Maia wrapped her arms around the goblins' neck, hugging him as tightly as she could even as she felt the blade slice through her throat.

She released the sun inside her, and it burst through her like an exploding star.

Together, Maia and the goblin melted in a flash of light.

A WORLD WITH NO GOODBYES

The baby took a deep breath and let it out in a wail, loud and piercing. It echoed through the trees, shaking the late summer leaves on the branches.

It was the most beautiful sound Cerelia had ever heard.

"Hush now, darling; don't you cry. I'll give you the world of the sun and sky." Cerelia wrapped the little girl in a blanket she found buried in the torn-up vines of the cottage. Not everything had burned, but the gargoyle and her nest were gone, along with the thatch roof and most of Cerelia's books.

That was okay. Those were all things she didn't need now that she had the child.

Maia's child.

Her child. For within the little body made of rampion and the last of her own daughter's remains beat Cerelia's own heart.

The surge of power that had come with having her heart in a flesh and blood body rather than deep in the earth was intoxicating. Her wounds had stitched themselves together in a moment, her limbs stronger than any rumple goblin.

And she could feel the tiniest shift in the green things of

the forest, as if the life force of every plant flowed in through her and back out again. Beneath her feet, the garden was waking and regrowing, sending tiny shoots up through the ash. It was never-ending and she was a part of it.

You are more powerful than you believe.

That power surged in every cell in Cerelia's body.

Wrapped tightly, the little girl stopped crying and sucked on her fingers.

"You will grow to be the most beautiful creature in the enchanted forest. You will be wise and kind and curious." Cerelia smiled at the child in her arms. "And you will be mine. I will be your *Gothel*, forever and always."

Around them, the world started to glow.

Cerelia looked up.

Tears of Midnight drifted up from the ground. The seeds had been sleeping ever since the night Cerelia had surprised Maia beneath the full moon. The look of delight on the girl's face had been priceless, and Cerelia's chest tightened in sadness at the memory.

She wished she had been powerful enough to save Maia, too. To defeat Six and the rumples who destroyed her home and took the only person she had loved in over a century. That regret would always live as an ache in her bones.

But at least she had been able to give Maia a final gift. Cerelia would never know but would always believe that in the end, Maia had won.

The tiny glowing drops hovered in the air, spinning from their little umbrella of fluff. There were a hundred times more of them than there had been for Maia.

Because this child was now the spirit and flesh of all of them.

Cerelia plucked one of the Tears from the air and squeezed the moon juice from it into the infant's mouth. The baby suckled the milky liquid and then searched for more.

Cerelia fed her one Tear after the other until the little girl slept.

Looking at the baby's perfect peaceful face, with her long lashes resting on a pair of rosy cheeks and full lips suckling delicately in her sleep, Cerelia thought of the perfect name.

"Rapunzel."

With a wave of her hand, the vines bloomed to life and reconstructed the cradle. Cerelia laid her little Rapunzel inside to sleep while she sifted through the wreckage of the cottage. She collected a few supplies—an unbroken jar of Maia's strawberry jam, a pair of gargoyle eggs that had survived the fire, and some other essentials that she would need on their journey—and tied on the scraps of leather that Maia had used for boots.

With a pack slung on her back, Cerelia picked up the infant and swept her hand through the Tears of Midnight, collecting enough for the rest of the night. Their milky white glow dimmed as the sun lit the horizon to the east.

The garden would heal itself. The vines and the reaper blossoms would grow wild next to the dragonberries and the fox shrubs. The earth would claim Xee's carcass and the bodies of the goblins after the night fairies' young had eaten their insides.

Life would always go on.

Balance.

She kissed Rapunzel's perfect face. "We are going to live in a tower where you shall have hair twenty ells long and sing to the sea. I swear to you, Rapunzel, nothing will ever cause you harm."

Cerelia took in a deep breath of the late summer air and stepped out over the boundary that had bordered her world for over a hundred years.

CERELIA'S LULLABY

Hush now, darling; close your eyes;
Dream yourself a thousand lives.
One life of true love; one life of power;
One life of kissing crows
in a witch's crumbling tower.
One life on a pirate ship with chests full of gold,
And one life in a land where you'll never grow old.
Sleep now, darling; close your eyes.
Dream of a world with no goodbyes.
A world of summer; a world of play;
A world of wishes and night-cursed fae.
A world where the moon sheds her midnight tears.
And the salt of the sea washes clean our fears.
Hush now, darling; don't you cry.
I'll give you the world of the sun and sky.

KISSING CROWS

C.M. ADLER

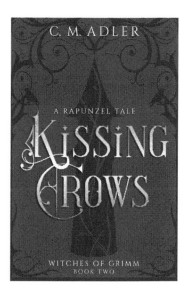

Once upon a time, there was a beautiful, curious girl who lived in an enchanted forest by the sea. Her mother loved her so much that she kept her in a tower, safe from anything that might ever harm her. And it was there, beneath the bright spring sun, that the girl wished she was free to fly with the crows...

ABOUT THE AUTHOR

CM Adler is the thriller and dark fantasy name for award-winning author Christine Nielson. Christine lives a life that's certainly never boring, and if there is ever a dull moment, she fills it with more writing projects.

Nestled in the mountains of northern Utah, Christine spends her days with her three human children and her additional four-legged, furry brood. In a former life, Christine taught English and karate and developed a love of spinning fire. Follow her adventures through her newsletter.

facebook.com/CMAdlerAuthor
twitter.com/CMAdler9
instagram.com/christinenielson_cmadler

Made in the USA
Coppell, TX
02 October 2021

63344207R00104